**Praise for *Milk Blood Heat***

"Electric . . . a tapestry of intimate moments punctuated by Moniz's tight, uncompromising prose."
—*Time*

"Like snow in the Sunshine State—'There was a sense of betrayal in it. Like how dare Florida, of all places, try and turn a season'—the short stories in Moniz's first collection constantly surprise. In unvarnished, visceral prose, Moniz uses the 'swampy stench' of Florida as a backdrop to explore the internal and external perfidies of womanhood."
—*O Magazine*, "20 of the Best Books of February 2021 to Fall in Love With"

"Mortality is the undercurrent in Dantiel W. Moniz's electrifying debut story collection, *Milk Blood Heat*, but where there's death there is the whir of life, too . . . Reading one of Moniz's stories is like holding your breath underwater while letting the salt sting your fresh wounds. It's exhilarating and shocking and even healing. The power in these stories rests in their veracity, vitality and vulnerability."
—*Washington Post*

"Moniz's characters are survivors. Throughout the book, they endure and absorb the losses of those around them . . . The easy pleasures which Florida offers in vast supply also come with a cost. Where others may sail past the price, Moniz makes it her focus. Actions mean more than words, but as a writer, Moniz knows that words are the connective tissue that give us the faith we need to carry on. How she illuminates that reasoning through direct and unwavering language is downright magical."
—*Boston Globe*

"The women and girls who populate Floridian author Dantiel W. Moniz's outstanding literary debut, *Milk Blood Heat*, are perched precariously on the razor-thin edge of something big: adulthood, motherhood, infidelity, love, loss, death . . . Moniz pulls back the curtain on some of the more intimate complexities of the female experience and exposes it in all its messy splendor." —*Atlanta Journal Constitution*

"Set against the lush and unpredictable backdrop of Florida, these 11 stories present women and girls as we really are: complex, deep, smart, sour, joyful, tough, loving and powerful."
—*Ms. Magazine*

"Life's inflection points, mundane but universal, mark the Black and brown Floridians who populate these stories . . . But in Moniz's collection, the ordinary experience of being female is laced with a kind of enchantment . . . Entire stories seem bathed in a warm radiance . . . One can glow with both love and rage." —*New York Times*

"The stories in Moniz's debut collection—many of which shine a multihued light on Black girlhood in Florida—are to not only be read but felt. Like Danielle Evans and Lauren Groff, Moniz is unafraid to expose the darkened corners of the Sunshine State, and of female desire." —*O Magazine*

"If the 'Florida Man' memes pulled from years of headlines have taught us anything, it's that the Sunshine State is its own world, unique from any other American region. In enchanting prose, debut storyteller Dantiel W. Moniz plunges readers head first into the lives of oft misunderstood Floridians and their personal crises, stitching together a portrait that feels both original and startlingly familiar." —*Elle*

"These dark, emotional stories show a variety of characters at critical moments in their lives. Moniz focuses particularly on the crossroads of girlhood, and her stories refuse to provide neat, tidy endings." —*Book Riot*

"Dantiel Moniz's sparkling debut story collection, *Milk Blood Heat*, is vibrant and alive, full of energy and desire and with a sharp focus on the body . . . In this collection, we get to see the whole, the mind and body fitting together, in striking stories brimming with life." —*Ploughshares*

"Visceral, corporeal, evocative of something as comforting as it is disturbing . . . explores the myriad messy ways people—siblings, cousins, mothers, daughters—love, or try to love, each other in prose that is both nuanced and so lush you can taste it." —*Shondaland*

"Moniz writes about family, marriage, class, loss, and race with wisdom and intimacy, and her stories are rife with images and sentences that can stand strikingly alone . . . All of the stories here are boldly told and hum with tension."
—*The Rumpus*

"As its title suggests, this book's 11 stories are about human need, about intimacy physical and otherwise, and about what happens when it fails." —*Tampa Bay Times*

"These stories are fire . . . This debut collection has staying power, will prove a joy for anyone who loves short stories, and deserves close study . . . *Milk Blood Heat* should be one of the collections we're discussing, teaching, and rereading for years to come." —*Chicago Review of Books*

"Black and Latinx girls and women in Florida are the main characters in Dantiel Moniz's thrilling debut story collection. Not-yet-girls, not-yet-women traffic not in princess dresses but in guts and risk. You think writing about menstruation is taboo? What about little girl characters literally drinking blood? Moniz serves up a feast for anyone ready to move beyond the 'sugar and spice and everything nice' lie."—*Glamour*

"Characters wade through family obligations, and personal contradictions in this collection of short stories set in the sunshine state. Study the intergenerational struggles of a group of people fighting to define themselves in North Florida and be forced to think twice before shaming their choices." —*Essence*

"A fresh feel for the intensity and contradictions of girlhood sings across tough stories . . . The prose is pretty, but it punishes." —*Entertainment Weekly*

"*Milk Blood Heat* is a hypnotizing revelation . . . characters on the brink of change consider the fugitive qualities of darkness and light, how they play both against and with one another, alternately freeing and restricting . . . a beautifully unsettling gospel of light and dark, declaring 'you could be both things and still be loved' . . . an incandescent and rebellious arrival." —*Shelf Awareness*

"There's something about this book that excites me, about the possibility of form and collections that take on different modes while still feeling cohesive."

—Danielle Evans, *New York* magazine

"In Moniz's debut collection, girls seethe and women scorn in the houses and bars and schoolyards of Florida . . . Every story in this book feels soaked with heat and blood and wanting and a slice—sometimes more—of danger." —*Literary Hub*

"The unyielding pressure with which Dantiel W. Moniz shocks her stories makes *Milk Blood Heat* a singularly terrifying and unmissable work of contemporary fiction—one that subverts the myths of pious girlhood in cunning, unforeseeable ways."
—*Paperback Paris*

"The stories in *Milk Blood Heat* are glorious. We meet an eclectic cast of Floridians grappling with questions of what it is to be human and how to live in the world: difference, girlhood, womanhood, manhood, pleasure, loss, and the visceral desire to belong. The prose pulsates with wonderment, easing us into moments of discovery that surprise, and deepen, both our and the characters' sense of the world. I enjoyed, particularly, the ways in which these stories are filled with incisive bursts of ecstasy, broadening our experience of joy and heartache."
—Novuyo Rosa Tshuma, *The Millions*, "A Year in Reading"

"Exquisitely written . . . Moniz's luscious prose pulls the readers into a world they've probably never inhabited even though they're set in one of the country's most populous states . . . Like your favorite album: you don't want to skip a track." —*Debutiful*

"Moniz has won multiple awards for her individual stories, and this excellent debut collection shows why . . . She nails aching moments of naked human emotion in direct if luscious language . . . While many story collections suffer from a sameness of theme, character, or plot, that's not a problem here. The tales are generally set in Florida, but the similarities end there; each entry is distinctive in its premise, and each will surprise the reader in a different way. What gives the collection coherence is Moniz's distinctive vision. VERDICT: Highly recommended; catch this writer early in her game."

—*Library Journal* (starred review)

"This powerful debut collection is a wonderland of deep female characters navigating their lives against the ever changeable backdrop of Florida. The feminine is sublime throughout these stories, featuring girls and women who are submerged in loss, love, death, temptation, and the cruelty and benevolence of motherhood, two sides of the same coin. Each story vibrates with a thrumming undercurrent of primal power, found in both nature and in the most shadowy parts of ourselves . . . Dark and lushly layered, these stories will bewitch you."

—*Kirkus Reviews* (starred review)

"Each of the stories in this collection is anchored by Moniz's gorgeous, precise prose . . . Though they share certain geographic and thematic connections, the tales are quite diverse in their perspectives and casts. What unites them, and what keeps us turning the pages through scenes of tragedy and self-discovery, rebellion and reconciliation, trauma and agency, is the singular voice guiding each character. In nearly every paragraph, Moniz unfurls some new observation that nestles down in your brain and sits, steeping like tea leaves, until each story has formed a cohesive, powerful emotional experience. It's a magical sensation that reveals astonishing talent. *Milk Blood Heat* is a slim but mighty volume of short fiction, one that announces Moniz as a transfixing voice capable of limning often staggering emotional truths."

—*BookPage* (starred review)

"Sublime . . . Dantiel W. Moniz explores love and loss with grace." —Adam Vitcavage, *Electric Literature*

"Each story is filled with such vivid detail and a clear sense of character; you'll never want them to run out." —*Alma*

"Northern Florida looms large over the 11 stories that comprise Moniz's smart debut collection, a comingling of themes of adolescent discovery, family strain, and temptation's dangerous appeal . . . Moniz knows her characters well and writes with confidence throughout, letting narratives meander without losing sight of their destinations. Each of these humanity-studying journeys through the Sunshine State easily stands on its own." —*Publishers Weekly*

"Fascinating . . . [the stories'] connective moments are both unpredictable and earned . . . This story collection is for readers who want to be both challenged and compelled."

—*Booklist*

"*Milk Blood Heat* is a seething excavation of want and human error. Moniz writes about the hard incongruities of intimacy with great urgency and tenderness."

—Raven Leilani, author of *Luster*

"Dantiel W. Moniz sings of Florida, girlhood, family, loss, and the glorious, ecstatic, devastating human body. A gorgeous debut from a wickedly talented new writer."

—Lauren Groff, author of *Florida*

"The stories in this book are rigorous and complex, lush and surprising. They are visceral, full of the intimate awe of existing in flesh. A wonder of a debut."

—Nana Kwame Adjei-Brenyah, author of *Friday Black*

"These stories and the characters that drive them are like lightning—spectacular, beautiful, carrying a hint of danger. Dantiel Moniz is a brilliant new talent, her writing lush and sharp, her landscape so rich it feels we could step into it, her characters so alive and full of longing that they might step off the page and take the reader with them wherever they're headed next. *Milk Blood Heat* is a stunning and important debut."

—Danielle Evans, author of *Before You Suffocate Your Own Fool Self*

"The stories in this memorable debut have the mood of late summer evenings, sultry and dark, thick with the heat of minds and bodies engaged in sin and transgression, suffused with complicated desire, boldness, and shame. I suggest you pay attention to this book and to this voice, wherever it goes on to take us. With this cast of lovable, heartbreaking characters, Dantiel Moniz is announcing her incredible range and sensitivity, as well as her fearlessness in looking squarely at our human condition, in all its raggedness and beauty."

—Jamel Brinkley, author of *A Lucky Man*

"Wild and lush, *Milk Blood Heat* is teeming with complex women and girls: the contours of their relationships, their fears, their many desires. Moniz mesmerizes and unnerves in prose so precise and decadent it rises to incantation."

—Kimberly King Parsons, author of *Black Light*

"There's a comfort and a piercing in these stories, a prickling on the skin, an astutely honest gaze sometimes searing through places and emotions I both wanted to escape and to linger with. Moniz has crafted a stunning debut collection of stories with living, pinprickly prose, like a hot Florida day or a finger traced up the back . . . at once otherworldly and completely real." —Nafissa Thompson-Spires, author of *Heads of the Colored People*

"A collection for the ages, incandescent and seething. Equal parts grief, violence, and want, and you'll be glad for this jagged awakening." —T Kira Madden, author of *Long Live the Tribe of Fatherless Girls*

# MILK BLOOD HEAT

STORIES

DANTIEL W. MONIZ

Grove Press
*New York*

Thank you to the editors of the journals where these stories first appeared in different form: "An Almanac of Bones" in *Apogee Journal*, "Milk Blood Heat" in *Ploughshares*, "Tongues" in *Pleiades*, "Feast" in *Joyland*, "Outside the Raft" in *Tin House*, "Thicker Than Water" in *McSweeney's Quarterly Concern*, "The Hearts of Our Enemies" in the *Yale Review*, "Snow" in *American Short Fiction*, "The Loss of Heaven" in *The Paris Review*, and "Necessary Bodies" in *One Story*.

*Published simultaneously in Canada*
*Printed in Canada*

First Grove Atlantic hardcover edition: February 2021
First Grove Atlantic paperback edition: February 2022

This book was set in 11.5-pt. Scala LF
by Alpha Design & Composition of Pittsfield, NH

Library of Congress Cataloging-in-Publication data
is available for this title.

ISBN 978-0-8021-5944-1
eISBN 978-0-8021-5816-1

Grove Press
an imprint of Grove Atlantic
154 West 14th Street
New York, NY 10011

Distributed by Publishers Group West

groveatlantic.com

22 23 24 25 10 9 8 7 6 5 4 3 2 1

For my mother. For Jason.

And for all of us still finding our way.

Half gods are worshipped in wine and flowers.
Real gods require blood.

—Zora Neale Hurston,
*Their Eyes Were Watching God*

# Contents

# Milk Blood Heat

## I. Monsters

"Pink is the color for girls," Kiera says, so she and Ava cut their palms and let their blood drip into a shallow bowl filled with milk, watching the color spread slowly on the surface, small red flowers blooming. Ava studies Kiera. How she holds her hand steady—as if used to slicing herself open—while sunlight falls through the kitchen window and fills her curls with glow. Her mouth is a slim, straight line, but her eyes are wide, green-yellow, unblinking. Strange eyes, Ava's mother always says with the same pinched grimace usually reserved for pulling plugs of their hair from the bathtub drain.

The girls are at Kiera's because her parents believe in "freedom of expression," and they can climb trees and catch frogs and lie on the living room floor with the cushions pulled off the couch, watching cartoons and eating sugary cereal from metal mixing bowls for hours. At Ava's house they are tomboys, they are lazy, they are getting on her mother's last nerve. Her mother doesn't approve of Kiera, but they've been friends for two months—ever since late August, when the eighth grade started, and Kiera came up to her during gym and told her: I feel like I'm drowning, and though there was no water in sight, Ava knew what she meant. It was the type of feeling she herself sometimes got, a heaviness, an airlessness, that was hard to talk about, especially with her mother. Trying to name it was like pulling up words from her belly, bucketful after bucketful, all that effort but they never meant what she wanted them to.

This is one of many differences between her and Kiera—that the truth about the two of them changed depending on which mother was telling it—and Ava often wonders if their differences are only because Kiera is white, or if there's something more. Something beneath the skin. This year she's become obsessed with dualities, at looking at one thing in two ways: Kiera's eyes, strange and magic; her own sadness, both imaginary and pulsating.

"Get a spoon," Kiera says, and from the drawer Ava grabs a large one with slots. She stirs the milk and blood until it is the desired shade, the pink of Kiera's lips, a soft, hopeful color. They tip the bowl up to their mouths, one after the other, sip-for-sip, until there are only dregs. They wipe pink froth from their faces with the backs of their arms and sit still for a moment, solemn in the wake of what they've just done.

"Blood sisters," Ava murmurs, feeling somehow stretched in time—another sensation she can't explain. She imagines she can feel Kiera's blood absorbing into her system, passing through the mucous membrane of her small intestine, assimilating until there is no difference between her blood and her friend's.

"Blood sisters," Kiera agrees, and leaves the bowl, spoon, and knife in the sink for her mother to wash.

This is the hour of reckoning, or at least this is what they shout as they flock toward the retention pond behind Kiera's house, kicking up grass and startling the neighborhood dogs into song. They drop small stones into the water. Watch the tadpoles scatter and count the ripples.

"Run, little guys," Kiera says, her voice small and high like an actress in a bad horror film. Ava stomps and snarls in the shallows; she's still wearing her low-tops, her socks full of pond, water squishing between her toes. She is Frankenstein's monster. She is a vampire queen. She is newly thirteen, hollowed out and filled back up with venom and dust-cloud dreams. She throws her head back and howls and howls at the sun, pretending it's a strange, burning moon, and that there is no other world than this one where she and Kiera are.

Kiera thunks down onto the bank, sitting with her legs pulled up and her arms draped across the tops of her knees, watching Ava. Her hands dangle from her small wrists like claws. She laughs as Ava poses for her, thrusts her hips out at impossible angles and squinches her eyes tight. Kiera pretends to snap photos with her hands, diving onto her stomach to make sure she gets the shot.

"You're a sexy monster!" she screams, swooping to the edge of the pond for a close-up, splashing water so that the droplets hang in the air for barely a moment, rainbow-colored. "Say it! Be it!"

"I'm a sexy monster!" Ava repeats, and bares her teeth. Kiera yanks her arms and they fall onto the grass, a giggling heap of girl. They catch their breath and wait. For their hearts to stop thudding, for the warmth to drain from their cheeks. They wait for the howling they don't voice to quiet. It never does. Instead it evens out, a thin purr that lives inside their ribcages and the webbing of their fingers.

Ava knows she really is a monster, or at least she feels like one: unnatural and unfamiliar in her body. Before thirteen, she hadn't realized empty was a thing you could carry. But who put it there? Sometimes she wonders if she will ever be rid of it, and other times she never wants to give it back. It is a thing she owns.

Kiera sits up and brushes the wet tops of Ava's sneakers. "Your mom's gonna kill you."

The girls continue on without their shoes, fleeing into the shade of the small wood behind the pond, bare feet pressing down into cool, loose dirt. They don't cry out when the sharp points of broken twigs or acorn tops drive into the soft flesh of their insteps. They grit their teeth and keep moving. They swallow pain.

In a clearing where the sun breaks through, they find a dead cardinal, red and perfect, lying on its back with its legs curled in the air like small, delicate rooks. "Don't touch it," Kiera says, leaning in so close the tip of a bent feather almost brushes her nose. "Bird flu." But they both get close like that, hunkering down, drinking death in.

Ava wants to trace her finger along the soft black feathers surrounding the beak. She is jealous of its open, hollow eye, the utter stillness of its body. Even its rank, sweet smell. She lies down beside it, her head at its head, and stares up into the jagged patch of sky. She imagines she's at peace. Kiera lies down too, and they stay like that until the sun sinks behind the pines, casting the world in cool gold and nightshade green.

When Ava's mother picks her up that night, her eyes immediately scan her daughter—looking for unplaited hair, for marks, for evidence of her wild ways. She pauses at Ava's shoes. When she speaks, her voice is saccharine, all her words crisp, enunciated carefully as if speaking a language she knows but wishes she didn't have to. It's the voice she uses for her answering machine, for meeting strangers in professional situations. The one she switches on for talking to her daughter's friend's white mother. "Thanks for watching her," she says, smiling, but her eyes are unlit coals. Kiera's mother is a fluttering, airy sensation at the doorway, something fleeting and cool against Ava's cheek. "Oh, we love having Ava," she says, and her cotton-candy voice seems like the real thing, so earnest it could melt.

"Why are your sneakers so dirty?" Ava's mother demands as soon as the door is shut and they are walking to the car.

"Why every time I come get you from this girl's house, you're always a mess? Both her parents live here and they can't watch y'all?" And Ava says nothing because words never mean what she wants them to.

## II. Games

There are other differences between them: that Ava is the prettier friend but much browner, so she is often overlooked; that Kiera bleeds first, getting her period in the midnight hours, waking up to sharp pains in her stomach and dark, clotted blood smeared on her thighs—that this makes Kiera a woman now, and Ava still merely a girl; that when Kiera tells her mother she is sad, her mother tells her to explore her feelings, and when Ava does this, her mother just looks tired and tells her, Child, go play.

So she plays. She plays at being drowned in the bathtub, holding her breath with her eyes open underwater. She plays at being hanged from a limb of the white-spotted sycamore beside her house, holding tight to the branches, her body limp and swinging, until she tires and drops. She plays the game of *What If*: What If I step out in front of this car, right now? What If I don't wake up tomorrow? She doesn't mean any of it, she doesn't think.

Kiera likes these games, too, but she talks about death like she has nine lives. As if when it happens, she'll be asked, *Continue?* while flickering numbers on a screen count down, prompting her to restart. The girls like to bounce questions between them as they label different kinds of rocks for Earth Science and play house with Kiera's dolls.

"How would it be to drown in a pool?"

"How would it be for a man to slice you up and hide you under his mattress?"

"How would it be to be buried?"

"Alive?"

"No, once you're dead already."

Ava imagines this last scenario most often, poring over it with the reverence other girls would their first Prom. Her final resting place: the white-lined casket, roses in baby pink. The velvet Sunday dress her mother would slide her body into, and the socks she hates with the wide lace ruffles like a clown's flamboyant collar. In truth, it isn't so much death that calls to Ava, but the curiosity of how her absence would affect the world. (*What If my mother doesn't weep?*) Would Ava's mother imagine her beneath the earth, grave worms crawling across her scalp, her still-soft skin and small new breasts, over time, turning to rot?

Ava and Kiera string the Barbies up with rough twine by the neck, dangle them from the DreamHouse roof. They watch the pointed toes twirl.

## III. Poolside

Neither of the girls want to be at Chelsea Zucker's thirteenth birthday party, near the end of the school year, but Ava's mother got the invitation from Chelsea's mother and told her she was going.

"You need other friends," she'd said, standing in front of her daughter with one hip cocked, seeming to suck up all the air and light in Ava's room. Ava felt cowed around her mother's bigness, and also bigger because of it. She wanted to kiss her mother's warm, brown face. To slap it until her hands ached.

"I don't need new friends," Ava grumbled, knowing there was no fight; she'd lost already.

"Baby," her mother said, laughing a little, cupping her chin. "You don't know what you need."

Ava told Kiera about having to go to the party, a pool-thing at the Embassy Suites downtown. Chelsea's parents had paid for a two-room suite for the sleepover afterward, and they'd promised Ava's mother they'd be just next door. Kiera had also been invited, along with a handful of girls from their homeroom, but Kiera's mother said she didn't have to go.

"Chelsea's square. Why do you think her mom had to invite practically the whole eighth grade? But if you're going, I'll go," Kiera said, sounding benevolent. "We're sisters, remember?" That slice of blood, sunlight in the window. That wistful, pretty pink. How Ava almost hadn't felt the sting as the blade cut her palm.

The hotel is one of the nicest J-ville has to offer, though the girls are old enough to know that's not saying much. Ava's older cousin used to work here part-time cleaning rooms—dumping trash, replacing tiny bottles of shampoo, kneeling in other people's bed habits while he changed the sheets. He said people were nasty no matter the star rating, and he didn't stay for long.

The pool sparkles wickedly, manufactured blue, its depths guarded by fat, reddened sunbathers who seem to the girls like sly gorgons only pretending to sleep, ready to tear them from their skin. Little kids splash in the shallow end, shrill and unselfconscious, and Ava thinks that everyone at the party—even Kiera—must envy them. Thirteen was too old to play that way, and too young to know what else to do. The other girls dawdle in the only shade, slurping fruit punch from clear plastic cups. Ava and Kiera slouch together on a single pool chair, the sun burning at their backs. They tilt their heads close and conspire with one another. (*What If we run away?*) They ignore everyone else.

Only six other girls come to the party, most of them scraggly things with early zits and bad hair who are just happy to be invited, except for Marisol, who is both prettier and nicer than everyone else and wants to run for freshman class president next year. Kiera traces an emphatic box in the air with her fingers. *Square.*

At Mrs. Zucker's behest, Kiera and Ava cram in at a stone table in the pool's courtyard, watching Chelsea's father march the sheet cake toward them, the number thirteen burning, how silly he looks singing through his smile. All their swimsuit straps are slipping from their shoulders, sweat beading at their hairlines, chlorine marking the humid spring air in a way Ava likes. They belt out "Happy Birthday" to Chelsea, who even with her wispy hair and chicken legs looks nice in this moment, glowing with her own importance.

Kiera and Ava don't really sing, so Ava has time to notice Marisol in her two-piece suit, how curvy she looks already, how her stomach has lost its childish paunch and flattened out. She keeps her hair long, shining darkly down her back. She's a woman already, surely, Ava thinks, imagining where else Marisol has hair.

"What a baby," Kiera whispers as Chelsea blows out her candles, referring to the late birthday. Everyone else has already turned the first teen, most on their way to the next. Kiera will be fourteen at the end of the summer, and Ava a couple of weeks after that.

"Zygote," Ava whispers back, feeling grateful for even this small advantage over someone else.

Marisol turns to glare at them—making Ava feel like a plucked bird—and claps hard for the birthday girl. "Great job, Chels!" she cheers.

"We don't need this," Kiera says, returning Marisol's look, though she doesn't seem to notice. The other girls cluster around Chelsea as her mother begins handing out the gifts, cooing about the smart wrapping paper, complimenting the girls on their good taste—so mature.

Kiera grabs Ava's hand and they stomp up to Mr. Zucker, who's cutting cake with a plastic knife, botching the straight lines so that some pieces are trapezoidal.

"Mr. Z," Kiera groans, clutching her stomach and bending double. "I don't feel so good. I think I need to lie down."

Chelsea's father blinks at them, and Ava sees him seeing them: two girls carting around perpetual grimaces the entire time they've been here—their sulkiness, their almost-adult gravity. They make him uneasy. "You don't want cake?" he asks, as if sugar and cream are the necessary medicine for any illness. An antidote to the dysphoria of growing older.

Kiera can sense his weakness like blood in water. She leans in close as if letting him in on a secret. "Mr. Z . . . it's just, you know, *girl stuff*," she says. The magic words.

Mr. Zucker digs into his pocket for the room key, thrusting it into Ava's hand along with two paper plates of buttercream cake. "Yeah, go on up. I'll send Mary in a bit to, uh, check on you."

"Thanks, Mr. Zucker," Ava says, letting him see her smile for the first time. She can tell it doesn't soothe him, and a part of her is glad. "I'll take good care of her."

They don't go up to the room; Ava knows another place they can be alone.

"My cousin showed me once when I came with him to get his paycheck," she tells Kiera. "There's a code to the door, but he told me they never change it."

"What's he do now?"

"Grows pot in Colorado. Everyone's mad as hell, but he says he's making way more money."

They ride the elevator up to the tenth floor, and Ava leads Kiera to an unmarked door that takes them to the roof. They can see their whole downtown, bisected and tidy, rolling out around them in unremarkable beige and gray buildings barely taller than the hotel; in the distance, the blue bridge spans the St. Johns and the handful of slender, glassy towers flash from the other side. Ava feels disgusted by this place, her home, but also exhilarated, as if viewing a world she can fit in her palm, where she is king, owns the light, and no mother can dictate what she needs.

The girls eat their cake with their fingers and dangle their legs from the roof, watching the tops of people's heads as they enter and exit the hotel lugging suitcases and their five or six kids, listening to the indistinct bustle of other people's lives. Ava can't tell if any of them are happy from way up here, if anything really gets better with age.

"How would it be to get ground up in a meat grinder?" Ava asks.

Kiera mimes flipping sausage in a pan. "Can you imagine? Someone frying you up for breakfast?"

"Yum," Ava says.

"How'd it be to get executed? Anne Boleyn-style? Off with your head!"

The girls go back and forth, losing track of the time, and for a few moments, it really is a world where only she and Kiera exist. A perfect place.

"We should get back," Ava says, standing up, "before they call the police."

"Gross," Kiera drawls, rising, too. She seems perplexed, looking out over the sparse rooftops like she's seen something but can't figure out what it is. She floats her paper plate off the roof and Ava does the same, watching as they waft slowly, beautifully, to the ground. Ava turns to go back.

From behind her, Kiera says, "How would it be to fall from a roof?" The image flashes in Ava's mind—rush of air, bones breaking, the red and lumpy splat. *Grisly*. She spins around to say this word to Kiera, but sees only the sky stretching blue—a real God's blue—overtop the ugly buildings.

Down below, someone starts screaming.

Ava feels her body being pulled toward the ledge. Kiera's name is stuck in her throat, her lungs shrinking, blood rushing to her head like the fluttering of wings. Her feet move without her consent as two contrary wants rise up inside her: the want to run, and also to see everything.

Ava leans over the edge, and looks.

## IV. Q&A

Q: Why?

And beneath that question, only others. Some of it meant, but all of it grief.

What were you doing on the roof? How did you get up there? (Didn't I raise you with more sense than that?) Did she say that she was sad? Was it something we did? Was she mad at us? How could this happen? (Why weren't you being watched?) Did you two get in a fight, did you *push* her? (You're accusing *my* daughter?) What are we supposed to think? Why didn't you stop her? (How could she?) Why would a child . . . ?

*How* could a child . . . ? Is this our fault? (. . .) What do we do now? Where do we go from this?

After the ambulance departs (lights off), after the police collect their statements, after anyone can finally move from the shock, they go home. Ava twists in the backseat, watching the hotel fade behind her in the dark. She'd told them everything she knew, except the thing they can't handle, the thing it's kinder not to say. That of all the possible and conflicting truths, there is a smaller, much simpler reason Kiera chose to fall.

A: She wanted to know what it felt like.

## V. Blood

She gets her period in the bathtub three days after they put Kiera in the ground. The blood is dark, more than just blood, solid red shapes bobbing on water. A low pain thrums through Ava's stomach and the small of her back, but it doesn't mean anything now. There's no one to compare with. The whole thrill of it was to stand face-to-face with Kiera and feel, for a moment, that they were the same. But Kiera was always first in everything they did, even this. Ava realizes while she has played at death, it's a thing Kiera owns.

Kiera was the one person who'd ever really seen her. She recognized something in Ava's face, something kindred to herself, and came to name it. (*I feel like I'm drowning.*) Who would know her now? Not her mother, whom Ava stayed silent with because if she didn't, she knew she'd scream, the howling erupting—an unstoppable, vibrant poison. Her mother didn't say this to her, but she'd heard her talking to her friends: If they'da spanked that girl every now and then, maybe she'd be alive.

Ava takes a long, slow breath and sinks below the water. She keeps her eyes closed as her body settles on the porcelain bottom; her heart is a constant thud, a sound as well as a feeling. It fills the tub—comforting, disappointing, absolute. Could she be like Kiera? Open her mouth and let water and blood pour in?

She opens her eyes instead of her mouth and there is her mother standing above her, watching, face indistinct above the ripples. She shoots up, swallowing water in surprise, choking on it. Ava's mother leans down and grabs her roughly by the shoulders. Her hands are firm even through the slips of water flowing down Ava's arms. She squeezes her and makes her daughter look her in the eyes.

"That's forever. Do you hear me?" she says, and Ava, for the first time since she's been thirteen, sees a flash of recognition in her mother's face, some bit of knowing. (*What If she's seen me all along?*) This new idea disrupts Ava, rattles something loose inside her, and the tears come hot and fast with the pressure of the empty emptying out. She sits and shakes with her mother's fingers pressing into her arms, and it feels so good to hurt.

"It's okay," her mother says. "Let it out."

Her mother grabs a towel and lifts Ava to her feet, dries her, and after showing Ava how to use a pad, leads her to the living room. With Ava sitting between her legs, she detangles her daughter's hair and oils her scalp, massaging it with her sure fingers. She braids the hair into a crown and all the while she lets Ava cry, saying nothing. Ava wonders at this new emotion, of feeling cracked open—like a small, big thing is happening inside of her, making room.

"I'm so sad, Mom," she says, and though this word doesn't mean what she wants it to, when her mother places both her hands over Ava's eyes, catching wet and salt from her tears, Ava feels like her mother knows exactly what she means.

When people ask what happened to her friend—whenever she mentions Kiera, recounting some silly thing they used to do, tame things people won't hurt to hear—she'll think back to gym class, that first time they met. When they ask her, How did your friend die? she'll tell them, She drowned.

In time, Kiera's broken body on the hotel concrete is not what she returns to when she thinks of her friend, and she'll think of Kiera often, especially in such moments where she is now and forever first and only—first high, first car accident, first sex. (That particular bit of guilt will settle and smooth into something like peace.) On her wedding night, she'll dance chest-to-chest with her husband—a man whom she's not sure but thinks she loves. A man who sees her, and doesn't try to tell her what she needs. Swaying close, their bodies generating comfortable warmth, Ava will remember a day near thirteen's end.

On what would have been her friend's fourteenth birthday, she snuck into Kiera's backyard and down to the retention pond to watch the sun set, water and sky burning pink; to stand on the same bank where she and Kiera had scared the tadpoles, where they had laughed and preened. The place where they—two monsterish girls—had owned the entire world. After the sun slipped under the lip of the horizon, Ava left the way she came, tripping up into the backyard, the sky darkening, all quiet until she heard something small and strangled cutting through the dusk. Kiera's mom was slumped in a patio chair in the corner of the yard, face in her hands, bathrobe twisted around her, exposing one milky, blue-veined thigh.

This is the image Ava returns to on her wedding night and many others: walking toward Kiera's mother; standing in front of the woman and placing a hand on her shoulder; how her mother's whole body seemed concave, as if consuming itself. She'll think of the way she opened the woman's robe and pressed her body into hers, their skin suctioning together where it touched, forming a seal. How she stayed there, silent, as time collapsed around them, wondering if Kiera's mother could feel her daughter's blood pumping hard in her veins—a howling, creating heat.

# Feast

There is only moonlight, a spill of it across Heath's shoulders, illuminating how he lies on his side, turned from me, and also the pair of miniscule hands floating above the curtain rod, the fingers small as the tines of a doll's silver fork. When I call my husband's name, my voice splinters from my throat and Heath wakes immediately, turns on the bedside lamp, leans in so close I can smell the sleep on his breath. He checks my pupils, then lays the cool back of his hand against my forehead.

"Do you have any pain?" he asks, and I want to swallow my mouth—to fold in my lips and chew until they burst—to keep myself from laughing. I place my hands on my stomach and nod. Heath reaches underneath my sleep shirt to test the tenderness of my skin.

"What hurts?" His fingers keep pressing, like I'm clay.

"Everything," I say.

He looks at me then, and in the look I can see him envisioning how I will be at some point in the future, ten years from now or twenty. I am a vague imprint of the girl he'd thought I was when we married, my mouth a black cave, ugly and squared.

"Rayna, you're fine," Heath says. "Everything's okay. It was a nightmare." He turns the light back out, and I don't correct him, don't mention the tiny hands that are still climbing up and down the drapes. We are both pretending. It's the only way we sleep.

This thing with the body parts makes sense to me, this fixation with scale; I blame all those baby tracker apps for that, measuring the growth of my child as compared to produce—kumquats and Brussels sprouts, pomegranate seeds, green lentils—except instead of roots, it was growing a brain and tongue, eyebrows, a thumb to suck. Briefly, I'd been in love with it.

Heath and I had been married for three years, and he had this whole other child, this ex-wife, a past life that had nothing to do with me. I had my friends' questions (*When y'all having kids of your own?*) and my mother's proclamations (*That baby's gonna have good hair!*). I had two hands held out, waiting to receive my due. I'd wanted a honeymoon baby, a curly-haired kid with golden skin and Heath's hazel eyes. While I waited, I would practice with his child. Out together at dinner, I'd wind a strand of Nila's hair behind her ear, tell her not to eat so fast, introduce her as *our daughter*.

Nine months ago, when I missed my period, when I confirmed with the pee stick and the doctor, when I told Heath over a bottle of expensive champagne and a card that read *Daddy*, I was glowing from the inside out. This baby validated me in the same way as my master's degree, my good credit; Heath's getting down on one knee. I bought the baby books, browsed the best cribs, shunned the million things expectant mothers should shun. Rule-by-rule, I was everything I was supposed to be—twice as good for half as much.

The baby was the size of a Washington cherry, with miniature sex organs even a skilled technician couldn't see, when I lost it. There'd been no symptoms, it was too small for fluttering, and when I went to the appointment, the milestone when embryo became fetus, the doctor told me she was sorry, her face solemn and practiced. There was no heartbeat. It was, and then it wasn't.

"This is common in early pregnancy," she'd told me. "It happens all the time. Once the fetus is out, and you begin ovulating, you can try again." *The fetus*, she'd said, and the word I'd been so excited about minutes earlier soured.

I opted out of the D&C and the pill, waiting for things to proceed "naturally." There was still hope inside of me. Doctors were wrong all the time. I prodded my slim belly, shook it, willing my baby to move. "Wake up, baby," I commanded, but the next day, the bleeding started and didn't stop. The doctor said, *It's beginning*, and there was nothing to do. Heath kissed my forehead, tried to fold me into his arms, but I couldn't let him hold me. I locked myself in the bathroom with the baby books, flipping through them carefully, and nowhere was it written how to reverse time or spark a heartbeat. How to make a womb worthy. I tore the pages out in handfuls and flushed them down the toilet, watched as they swirled back up in soggy clumps and came to rest at my feet. Later, in the shower, my baby would come out that way.

I saw the first baby part in a bouquet of marigolds Heath brought home that night, the small slit of sex resting among the petals—a girl. I was afraid to blink, in case it disappeared. She was with me, talking to me, which meant maybe I could talk back. I was glad to see her, even in this way; if a tiny ear appeared, I'd whisper into it how much she'd been wanted. But over time, these signs began to feel less like benedictions, more like blame. I didn't tell Heath; this was for me, and I didn't need a psychiatrist to understand what these visions were—a reminder of how the baby would have developed if she were still safe inside of me.

The moon has been replaced by the buttery glow of midafternoon sun when I'm woken by my phone ringing. I know without looking it'll be my mother or Heath. By now, no one else bothers to call.

"Hello."

"You're still in bed," Heath says. Not a question.

"Yes."

The college has been kind, allowing me to stretch the interpretation of "sick leave" these last few months, as long as the job gets done. I've covered my bases diligently: all accounts manned, no client left untended. Mostly I work from home, running formulaic programs that allow financial aid to go through so students can buy their textbooks and birth control, stock their shelves with Top Ramen. But Heath knows my primary post is my bed, my real work the practice of forgetting through sleep.

"You have to pick Nila up from school today."

I bring my free hand to my face and examine the fingers, the pinkish white of my nails, the frayed cuticles holding them in place. I bring them to my mouth and bite away the excess skin.

"Are you there?" Heath asks, and I hear an edge of worry in his voice, expertly mixed with a dash of irritation—our most common cocktail these days.

"Yes," I say, still gnawing. My stomach rumbles.

"Rayna . . . you promised you would spend the day with her." He pauses, and the space between us hisses with static, his wishes and mine distorted through the phone lines. "Please," Heath says, and I sigh. Now that I'm pitiful, I'm a sucker for beggars.

"I'm getting up," I tell him. I work up a spit in my mouth, swallow the torn-off skin.

* * *

I park on the street, outside the circle of mothers and fathers corralled along the drive marked for child pick-up. The children are hazy with movement, erratic bits of color sprinting from the school, waving papers, some carrying retro plastic lunch boxes, the kind I used to beg my mother for. Everything always comes back. The children screech like seabirds and collide with their parents with the same energy as waves meeting the shore. I shield my eyes and search for Nila in the crowd.

I see her among all the others at the edge of the curb, her tongue poked out in concentration, looking for me. At the sight of her, a pang starts up in my stomach, a kind of knocking, some feeling asking to be acknowledged. My hand is on the keys and the gas tank marked full. It would be easy to drive away before I'm spotted. I could vanish—follow the wet summery air down an unfamiliar highway and try to escape the little legs dancing on my kitchen counter, or the lungs the size of kidney beans wheezing from the nightstand. I imagine cracked earth; giant saguaro; the hot air drying the farther west I ride and the sun sinking red. Out there, I would track vipers through the bleached sand and lie beneath the moon's cool regard, my belly full and swaying with meat. The coyotes would sing my lullaby.

I pull the key from the ignition and get out of the car, cross the street, and hold my hand high. I wave. It's been almost five weeks since I've seen her, and I'd forgotten her six-year-old's exuberance, the brightness of her hair, that she loves me. She throws her arms around my waist, and her stomach, soft and plump, pushes against me. I hold her away from my body at the shoulders, look into her face, and feel nothing but appetite.

"Let's get some food," I say, trying on a smile, a stretched thing.

At the car, I buckle Nila into the backseat and she tells me about Jupiter's moons and clouds of space dust where stars are born. She tells me about gravity, how it keeps us pinned to Earth and makes apples fall from trees. "We did drawings today," she says, and promises to show me later. I know what I'm supposed to say, but can't. I am a dead satellite, picking up information but relaying nothing back. She's a smart kid, she senses this. She tells me she missed me, and because I'm trying, because I love her, I lie.

"I missed you, too," I say, and guide the car onto the road.

Heath and the ex-wife have agreed Nila must eat vegetables with every meal, a helping of fresh fruit and whole grains with little allowance for processed junk. I order bacon cheeseburgers and large fries at Wendy's and we eat them in the parking lot, sharing a chocolate Frosty between us, dipping our fries into it, getting brain freeze as the cold saturates our teeth. I let her gulp down my orange soda between sloppy, open-mouthed bites, flick away the bit of hamburger and bread left on the straw like a flea.

"Our secret," I tell her with a cartoon wink.

"Can we go to the toy store after?"

I recognize the hard bargain, the first experiment with parental blackmail, and don't resist. From the early childhood development books I'd devoured, I know this type of thing is natural. A sign of normal growth. At the toy store, I give her a quarter, watch her insert it into the crank of a dilapidated gumball machine and grin as the ball spirals down the chute into her waiting hand. I watch her mouth become a red ruin as she chews, her small, perfect teeth smeared with candy blood.

We do Nila's homework at the dining room table; she's still babbling, her mind a constant river, surging forward, changing course. Unlike her father, she requires only modest participation. She tells me that the only place as strange as space is the sea. Heath will be home in an hour, no more than two, and then I can escape this, crawl into my bed and lie naked beneath the sheets. I scribble gray spirals in the margins of her papers with one of her fat school pencils and imagine myself disappearing.

"Look," Nila says, fetching a construction paper cube from her backpack, pride glowing in the focused point of her face. The cube is only slightly smushed. "I made this." Its six sides are different colored papers taped together and each one bears a face drawn in Magic Marker and Crayola.

"Here's Mommy and Daddy and me," she says, rotating it so I can see. Heath's side is the blue of robin's egg and his eyebrows hover like two hyphens above his squiggle hair. He seems surprised to find himself rendered in his daughter's careful hand. There's Maui, her French bulldog, with a happy lolling tongue. I'm there too, depicted on yellow, my mouth a seedless watermelon slice. I could be laughing or screaming.

Nila holds the last side out like a gift, and there on pink, another body part. She's drawn a generic baby's head: there's a halo and bird's wings where a neck should be, and its eyes are closed, as if in peace. I can feel her expectancy, her need for my approval, for me to say *Thank you* or *Nice work*. She's waiting for me to be the mother.

I run to the hallway bathroom and vomit into the toilet. I do it again, and again, until there is only bile, the same cautionary shade as my stick-figure face. I can hear Nila outside the door, the fear in her voice as she calls to me and brushes against the knob. "Don't come in!" I say. I flush the toilet and climb into the tub.

I know I should go to her, should comfort her and tell her I'm fine, but I can't see her right now. I'm tired of smiling when Heath sides with the doctors, says we can try again soon, as if life is interchangeable, one indistinguishable from another. Right now I can't pretend that I'm okay or that Nila is mine. There is no make-believe that makes me less horrible, that changes the fact that all day I have wondered why Nila is here—her living, breathing, tangible form—while my baby is not.

Heath's home. His deep voice reaches me through the bathroom door, a soothing rumble. In the pauses between, I know Nila is filling him in on our day, directing him to my presence behind the door. He pokes his head in and when he sees me curled in the tub, his face clouds. I feel bad for him, but not bad enough to explain. "How long has she been out here by herself?" he asks, and I shrug.

"Is the house burned down?"

A muscle tenses in his cheek. "We'll talk when I get back," he says, and closes the door behind him. I can hear him pacing, gathering Nila's things before packing her into his car to take her home.

When he returns, half an hour later, moving with the heaviness of a much larger man, I'm waiting at the front door, ready for the fight. "Did you tell her I was fine before you dropped her off?"

He closes his eyes, moves past me into the living room. "When will you be able to let this go? When can we get back to normal?"

"Let this *go*?" I spark like a star in the night, feeling suddenly full to the brim. "I'm glad this is so easy for you."

"Jesus, Rayna! I don't know what to do. It's been eight months." He grips the bridge of his nose. "I'm not saying it's easy. I'm saying what everyone's told you already. It's common! It happens all the time. It wasn't even . . ." He stops. Looks like he wishes he hadn't come back. "We didn't even know what it was."

But I knew—soft petals shimmering gold, my baby girl. And I wanted my common pain.

"Maybe you never wanted me to have it. Too afraid to tarnish that pure family blood," I jeer, and Heath's face twists.

I can feel the thin line I'm towing, about to cross over, but this anger is delicious, satisfying as a last meal, and I can't stop eating of myself. "Maybe you're actually happy. After all, you already have your perfect daughter."

"That's enough!" Heath roars. He steps forward and grabs me at the wrists, and if he were a different sort of man, I can see how this might go. But Heath just looks at me like he can't tell who I am, like he wouldn't want to know me. His breath comes hard until the anger softens, and when he lets out a little whimper, a window opens, and through it, for the first time, I can sense his sadness, his jagged need. Stunned, I watch him swallow it. "How dare you," he whispers, and I'm ashamed.

I lean my forehead against Heath's and he doesn't move away. "I'm sorry," I say. "I didn't mean it. I'm sorry." I wish I could pin this loss on Nila, on anything, but there's no explanation, no one to blame. I know it's not her fault or Heath's, maybe not even my own. I kiss Heath until he kisses me back, until we're undressing and he's pressed close against my skin. We've needed this; missed it. There are so many ways to be filled. "Please please please," I beg over and over, like it's the only word I know.

I say it the way I did when the baby fell out, warmed by body heat and shower steam, the color of raw life. Red globules, liver-streaked, clots the size of champagne grapes. And then a slippery, silvery sac, small as a coin. My baby in pieces, fig-dark and glistening. Before I hunched empty under the showerhead, letting the water grow cold; before I slid the sac into a Ziploc; before Heath drove me to the hospital, I picked up my baby and cradled it, tried to see if I could make out a face or a miniature knee in the alien landscape of my insides. I rocked my baby in my hands, told it everything was going to be fine. I knew already what a mother should do.

Nila said, *The only place as strange as space is the sea,* so the next morning, I drive to the city aquarium and buy a ticket. The halls shimmer, filled with a dense, amphibious silence. Here it's safe to wander, to be driftless. I pretend to goggle at the flitting of fluorescent fish, to be consumed with nothing more than the wavering of sea kelp stretching up toward artificial light. At the tide pools I trail my finger along an urchin's purple spines and watch it shudder, blindly grasping until I still my finger in the middle of it, let it hold me.

Suddenly, the aquarium is teeming with children, a first-grade field trip. The kids rush in, trailed by frazzled teachers, their eyes wide and hands reaching, grasping as the urchin. At once I want to hold them, press their small chests against mine and feel that vital thump. The children awe at the boneless creatures resting at the bottom of the shallow tank, and their joy is simple, tactile, too much. Feeling unworthy of them, I fade away to seek out darker, more solitary spaces.

In a dim room where the water seems heaviest, I rest my head against the glass. For a moment, I can almost remember what it is to be unborn—this darkness, this weight, a comfort. Then, something stirs in the water, stealing my attention. In a corner of the tank, hidden by living rock, rests an octopus—iridescent orange with blue rings spiraling up the trunk of its body. Slowly, golden eye unblinking, it feeds a tentacle into the black of its mouth. Its other arms wave, two or three of them shortened, partially eaten already. I can feel its stolid regard, and like the body parts, I know this is meant for me. A synchronicity; something about ashes and rebirth, Ouroboros eating his own tail.

"Hey!" a man next to me says, a middle-aged father in glasses towing a child in each hand. He had snuck up while I'd been transfixed; maybe my engrossment brought him. He gathers the attention of a nearby worker. "Something's wrong with this squid!" Nosey, ignorant man; he can't even tell the difference.

I press closer to the tank and my reflection superimposes over the animal, my eyes a dark glinting on its body. The man is panicking, perceiving madness or danger—some invisible, toxic signal radiating across the current. But I know this act is natural, a truth beneath it, muscled and gleaming; I had heard the creature speak. Sometimes you must consume the damaged body, digest it cell by cell, to taste the new beginning.

I lean in, lips almost to glass, before the onlookers come to gawk, before the workers can interrupt this godly process, and look into its eye.

"Good," I tell the octopus. "Like that. One bite at a time."

# Tongues

Ms. Addler keeps a word-of-the-day calendar on her desk, so in fourth period, while Zeyah tunes out her teacher's prattle on American history, she learns new words: *censure, vicissitude, caliginous, exegesis.* Slick words, shape-shifting, Zey devours them, *voracious.*

Learn something every day, Ms. Addler's always saying. Her teacher is young, Call-Me-Katie outside the classroom, red lipstick and stitched flowers on her garter-topped stockings that show when she crosses her legs. Once, Zey saw her French-kiss a man after school, then hop into his nice car, her grin spread large as if she, too, were a high school senior, seventeen.

Today's word is *luciferous*, and Zey pronounces it wrong. No, Ms. Addler says, loo-SIF-fur-us. But Zey can't ignore the prefix. She knows Lucifer: fallen angel, Prince of Darkness.

Little horned man on the candy cigarette box. How could this word mean light? Ms. Addler says, There are all kinds of things "they" don't want you to know. She says it real mysterious, like some slim, blonde-haired prophet—but this idea, that word, quickens in Zey, growing big in the eternal Southern heat.

At home she takes her dictionary into the bathroom—locks the door, a blasphemy—to see what it knows about the devil. She seeks a different opinion than what Pastor or her family's Sunday Bible have to offer: *1) a proud, rebellious archangel, identified as Satan, who fell from Heaven. 2) the planet Venus when appearing as the morning star. 3) (lowercase) a friction match.*

At New Life First Baptist that Sunday—Zey and her brother bookended by their parents in the pew—Duck slips his fingers into hers and tickles her palm, their signal for boredom, for something funny or ridiculous an adult has said. Duck is twelve, still accepting of his nickname and blessedly silly. Zey remembers him small, head smooth as a pebble, her mother placing him in her arms. How sweet he'd felt, yawning mouth, breath scented with their mother's milk. He was hers in a way nothing else was. Duck sings along with the hymns, he always does, intentionally off-key, but this time Zey isn't bored; she doesn't sing. Instead, she watches: the collection plate going round once, twice; Pastor roaring at the pulpit, royal purple trailing from his arms; people asking for blessings, to be touched by the Spirit, falling out when Pastor presses his thumb hard between their eyes.

She listens to Pastor's words: Brothers and Sisters, all those who accept me as the Savior shall live forever in the Kingdom of Heaven! Repent! He whips the air as if spurring something invisible. Benediction or absolution—his necessary position in the power of such things. The congregation writhes. In the pew in front of them, Sister Ruth in her flowerbox hat slumps backward, speaking in tongues, this strange language flowing from the deep place where the soul lives, waiting for God to free it. The long, stray hairs under her chin tremble; her grown daughter fans her face. Others catch the Spirit, the Ghost licking through the church like flame. Pastor says, Bow your heads, let us pray, and Zey looks at them all with their faces turned down, eyes closed; the congregation, her mother, father, and Duck. Only she and Pastor keep their eyes open, and Zey examines him, the copper skin sweating from his exultations, the way he searches the room, bowed head to bowed head, as if measuring the effect of his influence. When his eyes find hers, Zey snaps her head down, too late, and doesn't look up again until the congregation says amen. On the drive home, Zey translates the expression she'd seen flash across Pastor's face—*supercilious, enigmatic.* Hungry.

After Bible study the following week, while her mother makes her rounds in her newest Sunday best, Pastor invites her into the cramped space of his office, which seems to double as storage. Boxes labeled "Christmas" and "Communion" hulk around his desk, and as Zey reads the words, she pictures their contents: Mary and the black baby Jesus in the manger; bulk orders of cheap wine and wafers of Christ's dry, tasteless flesh. She sits in the chair in front of his desk and Pastor asks, Are you godly, girl? She doesn't know how to answer. He then tells Zey how to be a woman—soft-spoken, subservient, devout, and clean. He reminds her about the history of Eve, how she took of the tree of knowledge, seduced her husband, and struck the entire world with her sin. How she doomed mankind to suffering, because she didn't know her place. Zey gnaws the inside of her lip while he speaks. A trapped fly whines in the window.

Her mother learned how to be a woman here, in the faith, and her father a man, but Zey's been to the library and looked up *real* history—slave ships and witch trials and women kept in bare feet. The books she borrowed were full of words like *pay-gap* and *redline*, and she noticed that in all genres, no matter literature or biography, men's fury stained the pages, sowing lies like white seeds inside of people's hearts. Pastor rises, squeezing around the clutter, and perches on the desk, his feet resting on either side of Zey's. He leans down and places a heavy hand on her bare knee. We need good young girls—God-fearing girls like you—to be the backbone of our church. Do you understand? he asks, and his fingers flex.

Zey hears Pastor's message and understands what's beneath it: that she can have hair on her head but not in her armpits; hair on her arms but not her legs; hair between her legs . . . depending on what a man liked. That she can be looked on, but not look. Zey stares into his face, her eyes filling, heart hammering in her throat. She says nothing, cannot move until he moves, will not cry in front of him. Finally, she looks down and Pastor sits back, releasing her. He opens the door for her to leave. God blesses you, child, he tells her.

Zey turns the moment over in her mind—at school and at home and even while she sleeps. For two Sundays, she sits stricken between her parents and even Duck can't break her free. What did it mean that Pastor, a pinnacle, the link to the Supreme, would bother to threaten her, unimportant though she is? He is Simon to so many: he says Rejoice, and they do; Repent, and they do. He says Pray, and the church goes blind.

For English, their teacher assigns *The Scarlet Letter*—the most boring book about an affair Zey has ever read. Her teacher asks the class what they noticed in the interactions between Hester and the town. Most of Zey's classmates only stare; they fidget and avert their eyes. Then someone says, They hated her.

Yes! the teacher booms, startling them to attention. But why? Papers rustle in the silence. Because she was immoral? another student tries, and the teacher cocks his head, his way of questioning an answer without claiming that it's wrong. Think about it as it applies to our own lives, our world, he says. What is the nature of hate? What's it useful for? And Zey imagines the townspeople, their whispers and cruel laws, their narrowed eyes. How they ostracized the woman, conspired to contain her light.

They were scared of her, Zey tells the teacher, realizing it as she speaks, and he jabs a finger in her direction. Yes! Exactly that, he says. Now he's getting excited, pacing before their desks, and Zey tilts forward in her seat, angling closer to his truth. Hate, he continues, is almost always a cover for some perceived psychological threat—our guilt or pain. Our fear. And how do we treat things of which we are afraid?

The moment with Pastor tumbles round with the grit of Zey's learnings, chipping down until her understanding of it gleams. After the next Sunday service, as Pastor jokes with Duck and accepts praise from her parents, he lays that same hand on her shoulder, and Zey glares at it and then at Pastor before she shrugs it off. He covers the moment with a laugh, but the hand becomes a fist at his side.

Pastor phones her parents that night just before dinner and though Zey doesn't know what's said, later she'll imagine him on the other side of the line spinning his lie, toad-like and sullen as he exacts his revenge. After she hangs up, her mother slaps her at the table and calls Zey outside her name—embarrassment, disgrace, *demimonde*. Disrespecting the pastor? What kind of example are you? Duck hides in the hallway, listening; Zey sees his shadow on the wall. Her mother says, What you do reflects on me!

Zey tries to explain, to defend herself against her mother's rage, her own coursing underneath, but her mother's so ashamed, so unwilling to see. She sends Zey to her room without dinner while her father watches from the living room, complicit in his silence.

Under the covers that night, her bedroom door taken from its hinges, Zey thinks of Ms. Addler, curled around the body of her lover like a snake, soft in her sin. She wishes she could ask her parents if it's better to be a sinner or a prisoner, but she knows now that her mother is afraid of truth and her father wouldn't recognize it, even if it invited him inside, offered fresh fruit.

Zey rebels against her parents for their failure to believe her, to protect her, in any small way she can. She refuses food, both physical and spiritual; she won't step foot inside the church. She lets their punishments slide off her back. Zey makes Lucifer a mantra, speaking the name aloud, blurring it until it becomes nothing more than the language of hisses, her own version of tongues. The vibration fills her stripped room, sinking into the walls and passing through to her brother, who is sad Mama and Pop now leave Zey home on Sundays. He overhears their confusion at her behavior. Their mother wonders if they should send her away.

Duck sneaks into Zey's room one night, climbing into bed with her, like he used to when he was small. Zey can feel him trying to word his question about why things aren't how they used to be: Zey packing his lunches with folded notes or borrowing Pop's car to run an errand to the grocery. He could come-with as long as he sat in the backseat, wore his seat belt, listened to his sister. Now, their parents hover like buzzards and only in the dark hours are they free.

Finally, he says, Why can't you stop? and Zey guesses at what he means—being changed, being *bad*. She twines her fingers into the soft mat of his hair. There's nothing she can tell him that he'd understand, that might bring comfort. It is the nature of light to illuminate, and she can't, like so many, forget what she's seen. She wishes this moment of connection was enough, but Duck's waiting and she has to speak. Truth is beautiful, she tells her brother, quoting Emerson, but so are lies.

Duck now understands the word *possessed* and tells his two best friends at school he thinks this is what his sister is. He describes how she lies on the floor of her room with her legs straight up against the wall, how that peculiar sound she makes glows in the air around her head like the letter 'S' come to life. He tells them how Pastor pulled him aside last Sunday and told him the devil came in many forms, but most shaped like women.

They are his best friends, but he is not theirs. His friends tell other friends until the word breaks out, and suddenly, Rylan stands before him on the playground, fresh-cut fade, fat lips sneering, his father's gold chains around his neck. His big hands hang loose as if just passing the time, the knuckles cracked and dry. He's in Duck's grade but held back—almost fourteen, dumb in his anger at all these smaller boys who belong.

I heard your sister's on some *Exorcist* shit, he says. Head spinning around and shit. Duck mumbles, tries to move around him, but Rylan puts a solid hand on his chest. Think that bitch can spin like that on my dick?

The playground erupts, Duck's classmates pouring one out for his defeat. Duck knows that, next to an insult to his mother, this is the worst a boy can say. He knows he can't allow this to slide, not here with all the other boys listening. He knows before he steps forward that he'll lose. But he does it anyway.

When her brother comes home from school, Zey, reading on the front steps, stops him at the door before she loses him to her parents' watch. She grabs his chin, makes him look her in the face. What happened? she asks. His cheek is already swelling, blood pooling underneath the skin. His eyes are dark on hers. They're calling you devil-bitch at school, Duck says, and Zey's head rears back; it's the first time she's ever heard her brother cuss. They say you're going to Hell.

Who says that? she asks. He says, Rylan and them. And Pastor. He pulls away from her, looks at her hard until she falls back and lets him pass into the house. Their mother fusses over him as she holds a bag of frozen peas to the bruises on his face. What happened, she demands, and Duck, ever loyal, tells them of the fight but not the reason. Their mother picks up the phone to call the principal, but their father hangs it up. Don't shame him, he says and chucks her brother beneath his chin. I'm sure the other boy looks worse. He winks.

Zey sneaks out easily, once her parents are asleep. Though it's dangerous for a girl to travel this way, she likes how a street can feel at night, clean, almost like she owns it. Occasionally she looks into the quiet sky, her eyes drawn to the brightest lights, and remembers how once in Science her teacher taught the class to tell the difference between stars and planets. Think about "Twinkle, Twinkle Little Star," he'd said. Mercury, Venus, Mars—the planets never flickered.

She arrives at New Life First Baptist some quick blocks later. In the dark, the small, steepled church looks exactly as it is: hollow, misleading. A stage. She knows the stories Pastor tells are ones he's learned from other men, passed through generations like a plague until they become mentality, these adopted laws from a blue-eyed, man-dreamt Heaven. She thinks she knows who Ms. Addler's "they" is, and what they hoped she'd never learn: that she is not second, not of Adam's rib; that her whole being is God; that Pastor and those like him will continue to shout from the pulpit, raising boys—her Duck—to be hateful and scared.

Zey unscrews the cap of her father's red canister and breathes deep. She's always liked the smell of gasoline—when she was a kid, her father used to let her work the pump. She likes the scent of something that can burn. She douses the outsized wooden doors and steps back. Thinks for a moment of the headlines tomorrow: BLACK GIRL BURNS DOWN BLACK CHURCH, and the ways in which this act will be misread; how all the white folks—some black ones too—will be so thrilled for an excuse to talk about self-perpetuated crime. She hesitates one more moment, and then she strikes the match.

Don't.

Zey turns to find Duck standing defiant behind her. He's in his pajamas, one eye a shiny black moon, the other swollen shut. He and Zey stand off, the match still glowing in her hand, the possibility of inferno heavy around them. Duck moves forward and takes her empty hand, and Zey lets the flame fizzle out.

On Friday Zey fakes sick, coughing into her palm, and her parents, tired of fighting, barely question her. You've made your bed, her mother says. Once the house is empty, Zey gets dressed, goes into the kitchen and spreads two slices of bread thick with peanut butter and apple jelly. She knows that soon she'll walk through the door of eighteen, pass through her parents' house into something she can't quite see but can sense the murky edges of—the shape of her future. She will pack all her knowledge, strings of inky words—*pansophy*, *verisimilitude*—into canvas bags and wear them on her womanly body, where they'll glow like Tahitian pearl, and when she leaves, her parents will wash their hands of her. Duck will send letters only once or twice a year. He will pen his love on cardstock; he will ask her how she is, but never when she's coming back. Zey will remember Ms. Addler, and make a point to study her own power, to see the shadows beneath other people's speech. She'll remember Pastor, and his fear. At times she'll regret not having burned the church down, but she won't deny her brother saved her.

Zey puts the PB&J and a bag of baby carrots into a brown paper sack. She walks to her brother's school and when she enters the main rotunda, it's as if time has reversed. Everything's the same as when she was here—the jungle murals on the walls, the slack-faced administrators. All the places one could count on to hide. In the dean's office she is all dimples and smiles. She makes small chat with the woman at the desk, who's been talking to middle schoolers all morning and is grateful for the break. My brother forgot his lunch, Zey tells her. Sweet sister, the woman says. What's your brother's name?

Rylan, Zey says, and the woman looks up the classroom, tells her she'll page him to meet her on the way. She starts to tell Zey how to get there, but Zey laughs. I remember, she says.

Out of sight of the woman, Zey drops the lunch sack into the trash, and when she sees Rylan coming toward her—chubby, swaggering—her smile deepens. The boy stops short and stutter-steps, as if about to break and run, before facing her and planting his feet. She asks him, Do you know who I am?

He jams his hands into his pockets and juts his chin. Yeah, so? What you want?

Zey drops one hip, lets him see her teeth. What I hear, you've got something for me. She knows what she looks like to this boy, frizzy bangs falling into her eyes, skin *au lait*—she is Venusian, Aphrodite fresh from the sea. Rylan looks over his shoulder, tongue working inside his cheek. A student on hall pass exits a nearby classroom, but otherwise, they're alone. Zey can guess his dilemma, his ego warring with his common sense. She sees where she should push. You scared?

Rylan kicks at the ground, and when he speaks his voice is a studied growl, the much lower register of an act. He tells her, I ain't scared of nothing.

Then come on, she says.

He follows her into a supply closet she remembers from her time here, where students kept their science projects, their volcanoes and model suns. It's dim inside, and smells of glue and something spilt. Zey pushes the boy up against one of the shelves, spits on her palm, and slides her hand inside his pants. He is hard then soft then hard again, and caught up, stays that way. His unwashed smell joins the other scents; his sigh is sticky against her cheek.

Zey lets him enjoy this a little, her hand slicking slow. And just when the boy thinks this is going to be something else—further clout with his playground friends, fresh material to use beneath the sheets that night—Zey's hand clamps around him. Don't move, she whispers into his ear, and the boy goes rigid. Zey squeezes a little harder and stares him in the eyes.

She says, Next time you fuck with my brother, I'll find you where you sleep and rip it off. There are no shadows under Zey's words, nothing hidden, and in that openness, the boy opens too, his fear escaping bravado and legacy to surface on his face. Zey studies it; she savors its plainness. So you understand? she says and the boy nods, because even in the dark she's incandescent.

# The Loss of Heaven

He weighed 210 pounds buck-ass naked; 217 in his leather jacket and boots, which he wore that crisp March evening to the bar along with a gold stud pin in his lapel. It was shaped like a spade, a gift from his wife when they were young, once she'd discovered how much he liked expensive-looking things. He wasn't handsome but his light skin, wavy hair, the polished gleam of his fingernails, and the bills pressed tightly in his wallet almost made him so. As he entered the Albatross he stopped just in the doorway, imagining his body filling the width of the frame, giving the occupants time to look and wonder who he was. The jukebox played the Temptations and threw colored light onto his face, and a couple of women at a nearby table glanced up from their pastel martinis, one sucking the cherry from her drink. Satisfied, he walked in. Hilda swept a dishtowel along the bar top, looking bored, smiling out from under her bangs at a trio of men at the counter, a pretty laugh spilling from deep within her chest. He chose a stool in the middle, with an unobstructed view of her.

"Hey there, Fred. Jim and Coke?" she asked, the start to their ritual. Her low, drawling voice pulled something tight inside his stomach.

"You know it, kid," he said. He slid his jacket off and draped it on the back of his chair as she filled a rocks glass with three large cubes of ice, so big they could sit in a drink a while before melting. In the few months since he'd met her, Fred often imagined tracing one down the contours of Hilda's spine, recording an exact ratio of body heat and melting points.

"No lime," Hilda sang, placing his drink in front of him on a square of white napkin she'd sprinkled with salt. "Start a tab?"

"I'll pay as I go," Fred told her, as he always did, and placed a five on the bar. Hilda disappeared the bill into her apron in one discreet, fluid motion. She never brought him change.

The Albatross hosted a quiet crowd on Tuesday evenings, a mix of suits, day laborers, and truckers with three-day scruff. The bar's aesthetic lingered somewhere between a dive and a lounge, sporting wood details and burgundy upholstery along with burger specials and streetwise games of pool on red felt in the back. Older gentlemen sat at tables in dim corners sipping rye whiskey, talking with other men about matters only other men would understand; some kept their hands high on the thighs of women who were not their wives—girls, really—who did not yet keep house and so still had inexact ideas about how the world worked and all of the ways in which they could be disappointed. The girls possessed a malleability, a willingness to be impressed, their cheeks, soft and new, flushing at even the most trivial compliments. These were sweet, bygone qualities the men wished to bottle and harbor for themselves.

Fred took a swig from his drink and watched the young bartender over the rim of his glass. He liked the healthy way her hips moved under her black uniform skirt; the deep brown of her skin; the way she talked to other men, her oiled hair sweeping forward as she leaned over the bar to take their orders, a grin under every word. He liked that she knew what a two-dollar-a-drink tip was worth, and that his glass was never empty. Hilda smiled every time she made him a new one, as if they shared a secret—as if she *knew* him—and sometimes her fingers would linger over his, creating heft and heat.

"Still good, Fred?" she'd ask from time to time, letting him watch her. Making sure he never lost sight of his importance. He was good. Fred lifted his glass to her, the bite of bourbon still glowing in his throat. "To beautiful friendships," he said, and when Hilda laughed, even that seemed just for him.

Fred spent thirty dollars at the bar before heading home. He kept the radio off, preferring just the sound of his tires crunching gravel on the road, the shake of the V6 under his seat. He'd bought the '85 Buick Regal brand-new—metallic blue with a racing stripe—as a present to himself after he'd turned fifty-two. When he'd driven it into the yard six years ago, his wife had laughed to see it, asking if this was the Band-Aid for his midlife event. "What's next," she'd hawed, "a mistress?" Fred had been offended. He wasn't old, not yet, and he deserved nice things. Now, he caught his reflection in the rearview mirror.

"You're still the man," Fred told himself, and watched his eyes to see if he believed it.

/

Gloria was on the porch in her nightgown when he pulled up, a cigarette dangling between her elegant fingers. Fred cut the engine and sat for a moment, flexing his fists around the steering wheel, trying to calm himself. It wouldn't do to start a fight. He got out of the car and hauled himself up the porch steps, leaning against the railing next to her. He studied her profile, the tufts of newly grown-out hair like shredded brown cotton, the petite ears and dished forehead, her angled jaw. The small triangle of skin beginning to loosen beneath her chin. The sheer nightgown slipped from one burnished shoulder and piled on the floorboards around her crossed ankles; it swallowed her. She looked like a child dressed in her mother's clothes, and in that moment, he loved her terribly.

The porch light glowed orange and flickered with dazed moths as Gloria let him watch her. She brought the cigarette to her mouth and took a long smooth drag. Fred imagined the smoke swirling down into the cage of her chest, every bone illuminated, turning what was left of her lungs the color of stone. She finally turned to face him, her eyes wet and penetrating in their dark hollows, and he remembered when he used to call her his little bit of Glory. He didn't know when he'd stopped.

"How was today?" he asked.

"Fine as can be expected," Gloria said, flicking ash.

"And the doctor? What did he say?"

"Fred." She dropped his name like an anchor. "It's fine."

He started to speak, then changed his mind. He wanted to shake her, grip hard into those bird-boned shoulders until he felt them snap, but only a monster would treat a dying person like that. Instead he held out his hand. "Let's go inside."

She smiled at him, but didn't move.

"I'm sitting with the night," she said, and looked over the yard toward the low edge of the horizon, still crimson from the parting sun. Fred's shoulders sagged under the weight of sudden gravities: that she preferred her cigarettes and her own company to him. That she had even started smoking the damn things again in the first place, and now wasn't troubling to hide it.

When, two months ago, her oncologist had hustled them into his office with his grim face and rattled off his list of bloated, ugly words—recurrence, metastasis, inoperable—Gloria had taken it, dry-eyed, her head bobbing as if she too were a doctor, comfortable with the impersonal language of death. He recommended immediate and aggressive treatment and Fred had coughed into his hand. "What are our chances here?" he'd asked, and ignored how Gloria's head whipped when he said it. "We're not worried about the cost." He wouldn't let this white man or anyone else think they were poor. The doctor cleared his throat, said, "Studies suggest that patients in this stage, with targeted therapies prescribed in conjunction with homeopathic remedies, and rigorous adherence to the plan—" and Gloria stood up and left.

Fred found her ten minutes later posted up at the car with her purse on the hood, pretending to pick dirt from her fingernails. As he unlocked the door, he'd given her a questioning look and she'd just shaken her head. Fred reflected that only *she* could look annoyed after hearing a scary verdict like that. Only she could be so rankled. The first time they'd gotten this news last winter, she'd climbed back into the car and bawled the entire drive home and he'd had to carry her into the house. Fred waited for this delayed reaction, but she didn't cry. Gloria said, looking out the window at the street going past, "None of that had anything to do with me. All that was, was two men talking in a room."

The reaction did come later that night as they ate dinner—smothered pork chops and mashed potatoes and peas—but not the one he had expected.

"I'm not doing the chemo. I'm done."

"Baby, you're in shock," he'd told her, because he certainly was.

It had been hard on her—the chemo, the radiation, each feeling more like additional sickness than any kind of treatment. They'd cut Gloria open and removed a lobe of lung, and now a long pillowy scar curved under her right breast, raised several centimeters from the surrounding skin. She said it was her last-minute souvenir, like *Haha, what'd you bring me back from Cancerland?* Forgetting the scar, the loss of her hair, the sores in her mouth, and the dizzy nausea and fear of it all, they'd beaten the cancer back. And just as they were celebrating, finally crawling toward something like normal—this. It felt like the worst betrayal, but Fred knew if they did it once, they could do it again. He repeated that, financially, they were good, just in case she felt guilty over how much killing the cancer cost. Fred was a provider—always had been, always would be—a retired car-hauler who had worked since the age of thirteen. Above all else, he was a man, and he took care of his own. No one could say any different.

Gloria set down her cutlery and rubbed the place between her eyes, and when she spoke again, she looked tired and patient, like some kind of martyr; he remembered feeling irked by it. "Fred, you're not hearing me. I said I'm done. If it's my time, it's my time."

He hadn't believed her then, but shortly after that night, he began to smell smoke on Gloria's clothes. At first she spun the usual line, it was others smoking near her, but then he'd found a half-full pack on the floorboard of her backseat. She'd been in the living room reading when he confronted her, glasses sliding down her nose. He flung the pack at her and it hit her in the chest.

"I guess you've made up your mind," he growled.

"To live the way I want to live?"

"You mean die the way you want to die!" and she'd said, "What's the difference?"

She was punishing him, he knew, and Fred's stomach seized at the thought of all the things Gloria didn't say, that she kept at bay with such inconsequentialities as "fine" in answer to his nearly every question. Fred was certain that she somehow saw everything about him. That this cancer, as it ate at her body, had imparted in her a kind of godly knowing in exchange for what it took. When Gloria looked at him, Fred could feel his wrongdoings bathed in light: his dalliances with other women, that he had denied Gloria children because he hadn't wanted to be encumbered by their need. She knew, too, about the mad money tucked away in a secret compartment in his wallet; about the disgust he'd felt upon first finding out about the tumor, at the weakness of her body; his resentment at swapping roles, when she was nine years younger and supposed to take care of him. And the worst possibility—that Gloria could taste his absolute terror at being left alone, the bitter tinge of his shame dissolving on her tongue. She knew he would be a coward without her, and he believed a part of her enjoyed the thought.

Fred went inside alone, trailing through the three-bedroom, split-model house that they owned outright and which she often said was too large for just the two of them. She thought he'd bought it because he'd wanted a family, but he liked the acre of land it sat on and the idea that he could own it. Over the years, he'd let Gloria fill the rooms with art and plants and rare books, since she couldn't fill them with children. In their bedroom, he removed his boots and leather jacket. He left his oxford and undershirt on a growing pile of clothes Gloria had yet to wash, then stepped out of his pants and double-checked that the ten crisp bills in the hidden pocket of his wallet—all hundreds—were still there. He took the bills out and ran his fingers along their creased edges, measured their weight on his palm. When he was younger and his older sisters in dating range, he'd listen to their mother caution her daughters any time they went out with a new boy, giving them money to hide in their socks. He'd never seen either of his parents so free with cash, but when it was his turn to court, his father merely said, "Don't get them pregnant." Fred never got the lecture or the mad money, and felt left out. What if he needed to escape?

Holding the money gave Fred a sort of chill, a pulse of irrational pleasure at the thought of getting into his Buick and driving away. Maybe he'd leave the swampy stench of Florida and go back home to the Tennessee foothills to live in the house his father had built. Maybe Hilda would be with him, riding shotgun, her luxurious, heavy hair whipping in the breeze. He pictured her red-lipped smile, her hand on his arm—and wasn't that the most coveted thing? A pretty woman content to be near you?

Standing in only his underwear and socks, he put the bills away and searched through Gloria's side table, as he did whenever his own fantasies made him paranoid. He found nothing—no secret money, no getaway plan, just an unopened pack of Virginia Slims. Her little sticks of spite. He would've liked to trash them, but it wouldn't matter. There was always another pack. Fred closed the drawer, then walked to the bathroom to remove the rest of his clothes. Naked, he stood upon his scale and closed his eyes. When he opened them, he found he still weighed the same, even with all of his transgressions nestled snugly inside him.

Over the next few days, Fred had restless dreams: Gloria hanging blood-spattered sheets to dry in the yard; Gloria standing before him against an empty sky; Gloria, gone, and the goneness blotting out the world. One night he woke suddenly, startled and lost, and flung out a hand to feel her beside him, her slight frame set sideways, precise as a blade. He tugged her closer and pressed himself against her, wishing he could push her inside of his body and make them one again. Gloria responded, pressing back, and they fumbled from their nightclothes. Bare, her bones bumping at him, the reality of her smacked into the room; she seemed proud of this ugliness, of what she was becoming. She latched her lips to his and Fred felt he could taste the sickness in her mouth. Repulsion shuddered through him, somehow spurring him on, and he entered her, overcome by the expanse of his love and disgust. He bucked beneath her, filling his fingers with the memory of her prior flesh. He moaned, "Glory, Glory, Glory," but the past didn't come. There was only this new wife, skeletal and knowing, grinning down at him in the dark with what seemed like contempt.

Gloria's panting turned to wheezing and she slid off him, coughing viciously, her body crumpled on the sheets. When she finally stopped and sat up, wiping her mouth with the back of her hand, Fred asked, "Any blood?" She didn't answer, but riffled through her side table for her cigarettes. His lip curled without his consent. "You're really begging for that grave."

Gloria made a sound, though whether a laugh or a cough, he couldn't tell. She dressed slowly, with her back to him, her spine pronounced in even that sparse light, but when she walked to his side of the bed, her expression was muzzy. Fred wanted to turn on the lamp and recognize her, his Glory, but her eyes kept him fixed.

"You know, the closer I get to it, the clearer I see," she said, and left to blow blue smoke at the moon. Fred lay there, awake through the night, wondering why she didn't seem afraid and if she still loved him, but he was too afraid himself to ask.

He started closing the Albatross down on Tuesdays, staying later to spend time in Hilda's validating company, to bask in the beer-and-vanilla scent radiating from her skin. He liked to consider that he was personally responsible for keeping her lights on, for putting food on her table. That he, in some ways, was responsible for the girl herself—Hilda's dependable goodness a reflection of his own.

* * *

Returning home from the barber on a Friday in mid-April, Fred heard the telephone ringing on the other side of the door while he dug for his keys. Two times. Three. He scowled as he stuck his key into the lock and hurried inside, tripping over his feet, cursing as he scuffed his recently polished shoe. He could sense Gloria moving at the back of the house and wondered why she didn't pick it up. He answered, breathless, on the fifth ring.

"Mr. Moore." The usually clipped voice of Gloria's oncologist sighed through the line. He sounded relieved. "I was hoping to reach you." A band of muscle in Fred's chest tightened.

"How can I help you, doctor?"

"Your wife was in today for a checkup, and I'm afraid she threatened to find another physician. As you know, I was highly against the decision to forgo radiation." He went on about his professional concerns, his responsibilities to the Hippocratic oath, his reputation. He told Fred that Gloria's treatment was a matter of limited time. Maybe only months. "I know I don't get a say, but I was hoping *you* might still convince her. Mr. Moore?"

"Yes, I'm here," Fred said, eyes sliding again down the hallway to their bedroom. "I'm sorry, doctor, I—can I call you back?"

He hung up and stood for a moment with his hand on the receiver, hoping, if he waited long enough, it would ring again and the verdict would be different. When it didn't, he trudged back to their bedroom. Gloria was folding clothes neatly into her overnight bag, a cheerful pink suede thing that didn't match the energy in the room.

"That was Dr. Howard, wasn't it? Shithead. You know he has me listed as 'noncompliant' in my files?" She tucked a couple of dresses into the bag. They were so small, like doll's clothes, and he wondered at how she could even be real. "I'm getting rid of him. I need a doctor who's on my side."

"How can anyone be on the side of something so crazy?" Fred said. She didn't need to punish him. Didn't the sinner always punish himself? He felt a stinging warmth gather at the corner of his eyes, and he hated her for it.

"Fred, you don't know how it was for me the first time."

"I was there! I was right beside—"

"You. Don't. *Know.*" Gloria came around to him and put her hands in his, but his fingers remained limp. "Do you want me like that? Dead alive?"

He just wanted her, full stop, but he wouldn't say it, couldn't give her the pleasure of seeing him break. He gestured to the bag.

"You're leaving." He felt cheated. There had been no sign; he'd looked for it. He wanted to ask her where her money was hidden.

"Just going to visit my ma and sister for a few days," she said. "While I still can. While they can recognize me." She had a flight tomorrow afternoon.

Fred had a strong desire to knock the bag from the bed. To scatter the clothes, to burn them, to chain her to the bedposts, and Gloria saw.

"You want me to stay, just say it."

Fred saw himself sinking to his knees, as he'd done all those years ago when he proposed. He could wrap his arms around her, rest his face against her hip. He could give her what she wanted, whisper *Don't go* into that stark, hollow place. But his pride, his fear, kept him from it. He cleared his throat. Stepped back from her. He asked if she needed a ride.

Without her hair, Gloria's feelings sat plainly on her face. She stared into Fred's eyes until he had to turn away. She brushed a few spare hairs from his forehead that the barber had missed and thanked him for his offer. She continued to pack. Fred smiled to stay standing. "When you get back, let's drive to St. Pete. Spend a weekend on the Gulf. How'd that be?"

"I'd like that," Gloria said, but there was no pleasure in the words.

It was busy at the Albatross the next evening, a noise and bustle Fred wasn't used to and wasn't sure he liked. After he'd dropped Gloria at JAX for her 2 PM flight, he'd driven around the city, aimless and sorry, until he ended up in the parking lot of the bar, blinking at the squat little building nestled against the sun as if he didn't understand how he'd come to be there, and then understanding all too perfectly that he had nowhere else to go. Shamefaced, he sat in the car with the windows down until, at 4 PM, he'd seen Hilda stroll in; then he waited half an hour more. Fred entered the bar nervously, his fingers beating at his thighs through his pockets. Paused in the doorway, he thought he might leave but then Hilda saw him. "Look at you! Gracing us with your presence on a Saturday!" she'd called, and he'd felt immediately reassured. He was wanted here; *she* wanted him, and Fred regained his swagger. He withdrew his hands and grinned, feeling like the man he knew he was. "Jim and Coke?"

"You got it, kid." The jacket came off and Hilda brought him his drink, and for the first hour or so, everything felt the same. But now he was sitting shoulder to shoulder with a group of rowdy, younger-looking patrons, all swarming the bar for attention, and every other sip, someone jostled him, making him spill his drink. The Top 40 blasted from the jukebox—unfamiliar simpering over synthetic beats—and he watched people gyrating throughout the bar, as if any open space were a dance floor.

"It's like a dirty club in here," he'd scowled when Hilda finally appeared in front of him. His ice was a pile of chips in his near-empty glass. He didn't like this Hilda, skin glowing with sweat, hopped up from the rush and all the young bodies, and too busy to see after him.

"Saturdays," she said by way of explanation and—sloppily, Fred thought—fixed him another drink.

The big man sitting to Fred's right paid his tab and left, but before he could be grateful for the extra space, another body took his place. Fred, irritated and more lonesome than when he'd arrived, told himself he'd finish this drink quickly and then be out the door. He'd make sure to keep to Tuesdays from this point on, and he smiled to himself, already imagining how he'd jokingly berate Hilda for the poor quality of her service tonight, get her feeling just a little bad and eager to make up.

The new man tapped Fred's shoulder and Fred saw he wasn't a man at all, probably just old enough to be in the bar. He wore a white cap over a tapered cut, a green sweatshirt with a couple of holes in the collar, and a pair of black Dickies slung low on his hips like every other youngblood in the place. "Got the time?" the boy asked.

First, Fred pulled his comb from his shirt pocket and raked it back through his hair. Then he hitched up his sleeve to glance at his watch. It was gold-faced with large numbers, on an imitation leather strap. Most people thought it was a Rolex, but he'd never spend that kind of money to tell the time.

"Quarter to nine."

"Thanks," the boy said, then offered his hand. "Antonio. Well, friends call me Tony."

"Fred. Pleasure." He made sure to squeeze Tony's hand good and hard, and a look crossed the boy's face.

"My pops always said you could measure a man's integrity by his grip."

Fred puffed himself up. "Your pops wasn't lying."

"Busy in here, right?" Tony said, turning to frown at Hilda, who still hadn't come for his order. Fred looked at her, too; she was down at the other end of the bar, laughing with one of the fry cooks as he handed her a basket of greasy onion rings. Her hand lingered on his arm.

"Downright shameful service," he said nastily, then to the boy, "What do you drink?"

"I don't know. Beer, I guess. A Bud?" and when Fred laughed, Tony asked, "What, that's too green?"

"Might be. What do you do, youngblood?"

Tony was enrolled in trade school to be a mechanic, which he knew was fruitful work. He said barely any of the kids his age even knew how to change a tire. Fred agreed that this was true and Tony asked, "What about you, sir?"

"Commercial car-hauler, thirty-five years." He didn't bother to mention he was retired.

Tony's eyebrows disappeared into the rim of his cap. "Wow, I can't believe it."

"What?" Fred said, ready to be affronted.

"My pops used to do that work. Those double-decker rigs?" When Fred nodded, he added, "That's real honest work. Skilled work."

The boy's respect warmed Fred like the bourbon. He could tell this one had been raised right; if he'd been a father, his son would have come out just the same. He decided he'd stay a little while longer. Fred signaled to Hilda with a piercing whistle that cut through the din of the room. She looked over her shoulder at him, her mouth parted prettily. The fry cook slunk back into the kitchen, where he belonged. "A drink for my friend. Two of these, on me," Fred said, raising his glass.

Hilda brought them both Jim and Cokes, her nose scrunched up like she had something to be mad about. "Get you anything else?"

Fred didn't look at her. He thumbed condensation from the side of his glass and wiped the finger along the edge of the bar. Then he threw a twenty down, letting his money speak for him.

They both ordered the burger special—fried onions, Muenster, garlic mayo—and as they ate and kept drinking, Tony asked a lot of questions. *Whereabouts are you from? How much did it cost for a car like that? A watch like that? A house like that?* The drunker Fred got, the looser his tongue. He told Tony he came from nothing. Not a dime to his family name. "And now I got that nice car. These nice clothes. I own land!" He slammed his glass down on the bar, the drink sloshing up the sides. "Most people don't understand upward mobility. Always got their hands out, asking for something. Not me! I take care of mine!" Several people glanced over, concerned or annoyed or amused.

Tony watched him, too, his eyes careful and bright. "Bet your missus is a knockout," he said and Fred's stomach lurched, thinking of Gloria, gone. He put his head in his hands and agreed that she was. Hilda came by with her dishrag, cutting her eyes, wiping around Fred's mess, and Tony angled closer to his ear. "Prettier than her, right?"

Fred snapped up to consider Hilda. If he put them together at the same age, Gloria would take the girl two to one. But Hilda had been good to him, barring tonight; they were friends! He wanted to show Tony that he still had a way. That he was still the man. He grabbed Hilda's wrist, pulling her toward him just as she was walking away.

"Don't run off," he slurred, trying to hold her eye. "Stay and meet my new friend."

Hilda laughed and tried to pull her arm from his grasp, but Fred gripped it tight. Her second laugh came out mechanical and strained. "Fred, you're hurting me."

"Just stay still a minute," he barked. Why didn't anyone ever stay?

"Fred. Let me go." The words plunked down, heavy between them. Fred studied her face and considered that she wasn't so pretty; it was just youth that made her special. He'd had a million just like her. Feeling superior in this conviction, he opened his hand and let her go, his expression snarled. The boy next to him looked on and heat flooded Fred's ears.

Fred watched Hilda scurry back to the end of the bar where the slinky fry cook again waited, posted up against the counter. She said something to him, rubbing her wrist, and the guy's dumb face swiveled in Fred's direction, his jaw tight. Fred downed the rest of his watery drink. "Yeah," he muttered to himself, "come try it, buddy." He stood abruptly and wrenched his jacket on.

"You won't stay for one more?" Tony knocked his own empty glass against the counter and Fred sneered. He'd played right into the boy's trap; he was just another nobody with his hand held out, and Fred had nothing to prove, not to him or anybody. He said to the boy, "Haven't I done enough for you?"

Fred strode from the bar, his anger a molten coil in his chest. The parking lot was quiet and dim. In this light, the building looked shoddy, unworthy of his business. He spat on the ground and vowed that he'd never come back. Fred reached the Buick and as he searched for his key in the dark, fighting through his inebriation and embarrassment, an arm looped around his neck; he dropped the key ring and his mind went blank. The arm flexed, and by the time Fred began to struggle, it had found a solid hold.

"You're hurting me," he gasped, surprised that it was true, but the grip continued to tighten across his windpipe until he felt his breath sucking distantly into his lungs like the pull of a stopped drain, slow and then slower. His vision grayed at the edges but sound sharpened—crickets whirring in the nearby grass, the highway's white noise. The steady puff of the man's breath. Fred grabbed at the arm, managing to turn his head and catch a glimpse of Tony's face furrowed in grim concentration before it—and everything else—faded into black.

He woke on the asphalt alone, his body twisted halfway underneath someone else's car. Where the Buick had been, there was only litter, an oil stain dark and spreading. His wallet lay splayed beside his cheek. Fred struggled up from the ground, his throat throbbing. He snatched up the wallet and searched through it, muttering, "No, no," as if the incantation would make this act undone. His license was there, all his credit cards, but the cash in the main pocket was missing. Fred closed his eyes before opening the secret compartment. *It's still here,* he hoped, but of course it wasn't. The mad money, his wedding ring, the Buick, gone. Tony had left the watch, not fooled after all. Thick with shame, Fred hobbled back inside.

"Call the police!" he shouted, and the bar quieted, all eyes turned to him. "I've been robbed!" Then, commotion. Several men went out to the parking lot, as if Tony might still be there; another led Fred to a stool at the bar, and the patrons cleared the way for him. A woman with a beehive updo and rhinestones affixed to her long, painted nails offered him her glass of water. "Haven't even sipped it," she said. Hilda, who had been pulling a beer, slammed the tap closed and whirled out from behind the counter, disappearing into the kitchen.

Fred slumped onto the seat, wincing as he massaged his neck. In the mirror over the bar he saw the skin there already bruising, purple rising steadily under red. The other patrons issued automatic condolences and indignation on his behalf. "Damn shame," the men mumbled, hands in their pockets, fingering their own wallets. Fred accepted their shallow comfort, feeling the slick bar top beneath his hand, and also Tony's strong arm pressing hard into his Adam's apple; the way Tony might have slid his ring from his finger, gentle as a lover. He wondered if the boy had let him down easy, or if he'd dropped him quick, all 210 pounds, like a worthless bag of potatoes.

* * *

The police showed up just after closing time, both of them white and jacked with blue eyes and short-cropped hair, walking in as if they owned all the hours in the world. Fred buried his resentment and explained what happened. Hilda wiped the same stretch of bar for five minutes, listening. The cops were writing it down and so was Hilda's boss, trying to look official, his yellow legal pad headed: Incidents. Fred felt slighted, and tired, and important. He told them, "He could've killed me," and paused to see what reaction this stirred in Hilda, but with her hair swung over her face like a partition, he couldn't tell.

The officers spoke with a few of the other patrons who'd stayed behind. Asked if anyone had seen where the man went. "No," one man said, pleased to be questioned, "but I saw him leave. The way they were talking, I figured they were friends."

"Friends?" Fred croaked, his eyes bulging in disbelief. "It's a crime to be nice?" Everyone started talking over one another, wanting their opinions heard, and the officers beckoned Fred away from the bar, into a more intimate corner, to ask their questions. He turned toward Hilda, opening his face to her, giving her an opportunity to return to him all that he'd paid for. "You'll wait, won't you?"

Hilda turned her back, organizing receipts at the register. "Uh, sure, Fred. I guess I could stick around for a little while," she said, but a few minutes later, he saw her slip out from behind the bar, apron folded in a neat square hugged to her chest. The fry cook's arm was draped around her waist, comfortable there, and she left without even once looking back. Fred couldn't help it, a raw little sob bumped up his throat, and the officers shifted their eyes. He kept answering their questions—yes, no, yes, I don't know—his tongue leaden in his mouth. The cops said they'd call as soon as they had something. "Oh, we'll probably find the car soon enough, stripped and burned in some abandoned lot," one of them said, a little too brightly, "but I wouldn't count on the boy. Cases like these are usually open-shut." They finished their report and offered Fred a ride home, and when they put him in the back and shut the door, he understood he looked like nothing more than a criminal.

Fred grabbed the spare key under the fake rock near the steps and let himself inside. A dense silence lay over the house, the click of the front door, his footfalls, all sound disappearing smoothly into it, as if there were nothing physical to his being. What he wouldn't give to have the phone ring right now, shattering that awful, accusing quiet, so complete, implying to him something eternal and dreadful from which he could no longer hide. Would that the doctor might call with better news, or the officers, even Tony—who could have still been a good boy gone wayward, who might have looked up his name in the phone book and wanted to check that he'd left him alive. Fred wished so hard he thought he heard a ring, and he ran to the phone, jerking it from the cradle and slamming it to his ear. "Gloria!" he shouted, hurting his throat, but only the dial tone answered.

Fred felt all the tears he hadn't cried with Gloria the day before rocket up inside of him like soda in a shaken bottle, and for a few merciful minutes, he let himself weep, needfully and gasping. When he was empty, this noise, too, vanished quickly. Fred wiped the snot from his nose with the tail of his shirt, then unpinned the gold spade from his lapel and held it in one hand as he stripped. The oil-stained jacket, his boots, his pants. He left his clothes in a pile in the front hall, and wandered into each dark room of the house, rolling the pin on his palm, the fact of his nakedness following along the corridor. In the bedroom, the closet gaped, absent of Gloria's blouses, her favorite pair of shoes, a purer darkness leaching from within. Fred went to close it, and when he crossed the mirror, he would not look.

# The Hearts of Our Enemies

It is the little piece of folded paper Frankie found in the back pocket of Margot's favorite pair of jeans six weeks ago that calls for a cigarette and this extra pluck of courage. She lights up, willing the smoke to hotbox the car, to consume her. For this next act, she must feel hidden. The cedarlike smell seeps into the cloth seats and settles on her. Lingers. She doesn't smoke the cigarette, just lets it burn, and it is a relief to be bathed in its secondhand qualities. Her husband—and he still is her husband—would be pissed to know she does this, and that knowledge is almost as good as any nicotine.

It feels so good that as soon as the first goes out, she lights another.

Frankie looks out onto the tidy, duplex-lined street named for a flower. Women push babies up the sidewalk, clothed in name-brand workout jackets and CrossFit trainers, dog leashes wrapped around their miniature wrists and the padded handles of strollers. They park in the driveways, bring in mail, brown paper bags of groceries, more children sticky with peacekeeping candy bars, their husbands' dry cleaning. These women with their endless arms.

A small thrashing part of her congratulates them on keeping it all together when they could just as soon let those bags fall to the ground—purple cabbage bumping its way down the hill, the dozen eggs blinking open on the concrete—and walk away. They could let slip the leashes, watch the babies go the way of the cabbage.

Sitting there, Frankie tries to hold on to a self that she still knows: mother, ex-smoker, lover of all shades of blue and the rare luxury of freshly churned butter, but there are newer, darker aspects she can't yet identify, layered with grief, guilt, and rage. To sift them out and individualize them would unravel the known elements, so she lets the mess lie. And in the lying, a flicker. Her own bare flesh stippled in sunlight. Hands not her husband's, the press of fingers against her mouth. Their ridges and salt.

She isn't careful. Ash falls from the cigarette and lands on the seat. Frankie licks her thumb and wipes at it, smearing a gray streak across the tan fabric. The car is barely a year old, and she has so many payments left that she will now make alone. Her eyes flit back outside.

*Nothing stays new*, she wants to tell the women, though she's sure they already know. Not their cars or clothes or bodies. Not their children, fat and smiling, still happy. Still in want of them.

Six weeks ago, she had crept into Margot's room, pulling the door open with the knob twisted far to the right so that the catch wouldn't click and alert her daughter or the friend who'd slept over. Every surface was covered with something—fashion scarves and mislaid jackets. Scattered textbooks. Lip stain in shades Frankie would not have been allowed to wear at her daughter's age, one the gleaming crimson of newly plucked cranberry.

Margot slept beautifully, of course, flung wide over the small bed—covers tangled between legs and one brown arm trailing over the edge, the other resting across her friend's stomach. Marissa was long and dark and beautiful too, wrapped in a yellow gossamer gown Frankie wasn't aware girls still wore for sleep. Margot wore an oversized T-shirt and a pair of her father's old briefs, ignoring years of camisoles and matching pajama sets crammed at the back of her nightstand, and she snored, her face half-buried in her pillow, mouth open in a ring of moisture. Her one visible eyelid fluttered, crusted with sleep that hinted of late-night talk. Frankie remembered what it was like: whispering about the pros and cons of false eyelashes and girls at school with false faces and how many sit-ups equaled one slice of cafeteria pizza and which teachers were fucking which other teachers and boys' names they said before sleep and would they one day be fucked too and would they like it? She and her friends used to compare their bodies in the mirror, side by side, so they would know what normal was. Frankie wondered if girls still did this, still deadened their arms and touched themselves as if testing unfamiliar fruit.

To look on Margot in the filtered sun was like holding your breath underwater, she thought. A tightness in the chest, a small amount of panic, but bigger than that was the wonder at how light the body could be, held up by all that matter. The feel of it touching you everywhere at once—the soles of your feet, the inside of your nose. How you, suspended in the deep, could truly feel your heart working. That was how Frankie felt, watching her daughter sleep. A little afraid, a little hurt. Exhilarated. She wanted to kiss the sloped forehead under which all those attributes that made her daughter too bright and difficult convened and pulsed.

She didn't.

Even in sleep, Margot projected warning: *Do not touch me.*

Frankie slipped from the room as quietly as she had entered it, went back to her chair in the kitchen. She wanted a cigarette, but instead had a third cup of coffee—dark Arabian roast flavored with honey and cinnamon. She thought of the crepes she would make for her daughter and the friend, a peace offering in the only language in which she was absolutely fluent. In the fridge were heavy cream and strawberries she'd gotten from the farmer's market that morning, sweet-smelling and dense red. The counter was floured and the griddle set on the stove, all of it waiting only for the girls to awaken. She needed to be busy, to fill the space with hearthy smells. To set her hands to useful work.

They didn't wake for nearly an hour. In that time, the cordless rang twice, summoning her to check the caller ID before answering the first call (her mother), and not answering the second (her husband). The message light blinked like an active tracking device.

At noon, she heard movement, the muted, musical signature of girls in the thrall of serious conversation. Frankie pressed herself to the wall to feel the hum of their words coming through, to know their vibrational setting, but she couldn't feel it. She wasn't tuned in. She peeled herself away and waited by the stove, hands clasped above the warm bowl of her belly. The girls appeared some minutes later still in their sleeping things, Margot's hair wrapped and Marissa's combed down and gleaming, her daughter flicking those precious crusts from the corners of her eyes. Frankie found herself suddenly overwhelmed by the girl, a creature once of her own body and now nearly eighteen and too big to sit on her lap or let go of a grudge easily. What a gorgeous thing she'd made. She tried to remember what it was like before her daughter despised her, the small years when she was revered as a Mother-God, and said to the girls, "Good morning!" though it wasn't anymore.

Margot's face creased as she crossed to the kitchen counter to riffle through the bread box, presenting her back to her mother.

"I'm making crepes," Frankie tried again, indicating the griddle. She felt like a game-show hostess, grandstanding to highlight all the prizes her daughter could win if only she could stomach one unbearable act of kindness. If she would just let Frankie feed her.

Margot selected an everything bagel from the box. "We don't want crepes." She still did not look at her mother. Her friend leaned against the doorframe, one arm wrapped around herself, looking steadfastly out the window like a politician, *Nothing to see here, business as usual.* What was a three-month-long cold war between a mother and daughter except standard operating procedure? Margot sliced through the bagel, bread catching on the knife like skin, and put half in the toaster. She started eating the other half, tearing off chunks and chewing sloppily. She didn't bother to wipe the crumbs from her mouth.

"Can you drive us to the mall?" she asked. "We've got a project." She kept her tone even, but Frankie saw the slight slitting of her eyes, heard the dare in her voice, and Margot's whole face like the bread knife, full of serrated edges. Frankie would not have tolerated this behavior if not for her daughter's blamelessness, if this was just another instance of teenage impudence and not a result of Frankie's own mistake. Margot knew this, too. The temptation of *No* was sweet, was perhaps deserved, but Frankie resisted. She knew what was owed.

"Sure, no problem! Get dressed and I'll drop you off. Need some cash?"

"No thanks. Dad gave me some last week." Her father, the good guy—or *poor Charles,* as she'd heard whispered at the bakery and over rows of thyme-stuffed sausages at the butcher's, once the story got out.

"Good! That's great!" Frankie said, her voice so bright it was sickening.

The bagel popped from the toaster and Margot seized it, ignoring her singed fingertips, and thrust the half at her friend, who shuffled it from hand to hand until Margot gave her a paper towel to wrap it in. They left the kitchen as quickly as they'd entered, back to the place Frankie couldn't go. She was struck dumb by the swiftness with which people could leave. How used to doors closing a person could get, to saying good-bye or not saying it at all and wishing later that you had.

After she returned to the house alone and put the griddle away and silence again settled itself on the tops of the fan blades, Frankie busied herself with Margot's laundry. Margot liked coming home to the warm, folded stacks on her unmade bed, burying her face in the T-shirts to soak up the dryer sheet smell, a scent of manufactured lilac and of being small and wild and unresponsible. Frankie liked picturing her daughter this way, and so kept performing the chore.

She stuffed all the errant clothes into a basket, picked up the jeans that she hadn't wanted to pay for because, brand-new, they were already ripped, faded, and snagged. She thrust her hands into the pockets automatically, searching for forgotten gum or pens or crinkled dollar bills. Up came the square of paper, torn at the creases from being folded and refolded too many times. Frankie let it lie on her palm, holding it out from her body as if offering it the chance to fly away. Then she opened it.

There were two sets of handwriting, her daughter's flowery, the confused mix of print and cursive most people took up after the third grade; the second writer had pressed heavily on the page, the letters swaggering forward like bulls let free from their enclosures. There were three lines of text—of which only one, the question, was her daughter's. The note was mostly in French, and seemed innocuous for the fact that Frankie couldn't understand it. All the French she knew related to culinary school: roux, mise en place; to her brief dream that she would be one of the next great chefs, have her own restaurant, Michelin-graced. This fantasy before Margot, before her husband's dream of a more available wife won out. Frankie squinted at the writing. Temple. Lights. Love? She could have almost let it go. Almost would have, except for those deliberate periods between the English words: *Every. Single. Time.*

She abandoned the laundry and took the note to her husband's study, which he had made clear how inconvenient it was for him to have to leave. His work, very important. His productivity would suffer without reliable access to a computer and he was paying all the bills, was she satisfied with herself? If Frankie could have afforded to replace it, she would have taken a hammer to the thing. Instead, she booted it up, and through its ordered slowness, the warbling dial-up, she imagined a white-napkined table set with vases of pale peonies, creamy bowls of lobster bisque, seared lamb with mint jelly, caramelized pearl onions to pinch whole between her teeth. It took eight minutes to connect to Netscape, and another ten to approximate the words:

*I would worship in the temple of your body / With the lights on?*

Every. Single. Time.

After some minutes, Frankie stood, went back to Margot's room, and put the tattered note back into the tattered pocket. She added the jeans to the dirty clothes in the basket, set the cycle, left it all in the wash.

The girls sat on the edge of the fountain. During school, kids called Margot and Marissa M&M, which they accepted without complaint, neither admitting the small relief in having even this dumb rationale for being constantly confused for the other. Marissa kept watch, and Margot propped herself back on one arm, occasionally dipping her free hand into the cool, dirty water. The coins winked up at her through the slow ripple, silver and bronze and moss. At every lull in pedestrians, she sank her hand to the bottom, fingers scrabbling against mildew-slick tile, and swiped up a handful of them. She kept only the quarters. The girls chatted while they fished.

*You and Drew make up yet? / Forget him. I've moved on.* And Margot had. She had realized early on that evidence of her own desirability was almost all she needed to be turned on, and when Drew had figured it out, she'd lost it to him earlier that year, after they'd hit the one-month mark. But she wasn't sentimental. She knew what they'd had was common, and men had been looking at Margot since she was six years old, so she could recognize it when she saw it. There was always someone else. Sometimes, someone better.

Arm in arm, their pockets jangling, the girls strolled to the ice cream shop and bought two giant waffle cones, one blueberry cheesecake and the other strawberry. The parlor boy, dull-eyed and monosyllabic, didn't comment on the wet change or its chlorine smell. He made minimum wage, gave free cones to his friends and girls he thought might date him; they weren't the first to exchange fountain money for goods and services. Marissa ate her cone guiltily, wolfing it down to make the evidence disappear, but Margot relished hers, eating with a spoon, letting the ice cream melt on her tongue.

After her father had left, leaning over her bed to kiss her good-bye as if she were a child, Margot decided she would no longer feel sorry for anything. *He coming back?* Marissa had asked when Margot described the scene. *Probably*. She didn't think they'd get divorced; that wasn't her father's style. He liked to demonstrate, to make examples. Margot thought he was just punishing Frankie, not so much for the betrayal itself as for his own limited imagination that she could betray him. *I hope he doesn't*, she'd said, and at the time had meant it.

She was punishing Frankie, too, but not for what her mother thought. Margot didn't care about the local gossip, the word *infidelity* traded among the old neighbor ladies like it was foreign currency, like their own husbands hadn't been creeping around on them since just after the marriage certificate was signed. Like they'd never thought about stepping out themselves. They gathered to pierce Frankie with their eyes whenever they could—another's shame being the truest spectator sport—and wonder aloud how a woman getting so large in the middle could keep a first man, let alone catch a second. "That poor child," they'd whispered loud enough for Margot to hear, "living in a broken home." She didn't care about that either.

Margot was mad because her mother had chickened out, hadn't actually slept with the other man, and because Frankie had told her husband about the little that had happened when no one would otherwise have known. Her mother had let herself be shamed, like a bad pet, her eyes cast down in response to the neighbors' satisfied viciousness, and now she followed after Margot constantly, ready to lick the floor beneath her feet. Despite her new vow, it was hardest not to feel sorry for Frankie, but Margot was getting better at it. After all, her mother had done this to herself.

She remembered, once, when Frankie made them squid ink pasta during one of her wistful moods, going to five different markets for the ingredients, spending hours in the kitchen, steam curling her hair, the pots and pans heaped gluey in the sink. As they sat down to dinner, her father accepted his plate in silence, then made a comment he must have felt confident he could pass off as light: "Wouldn't it have been easier to make a salad?" Her mother had not replied, but left half her plate unfinished. Margot had been disgusted with her father, and with Frankie for allowing it. Disgusted with herself because she sometimes agreed with him.

In all of this, Margot was mostly mad that her mother had wanted something and didn't take it, and the consequences were the same.

Could this happen to her one day, some man make her small inside her own body? Margot posed the question to Marissa, who remained tight-lipped on the subject of Frankie. They had made it a fast rule not to talk about each other's mothers, only listen. This mandate would serve them well, rewarding each girl with the other's loyalty long after their high school years. Margot finished her cone, and Marissa said, kindly and with knowing, *Enough moping.*

They browsed the stores, trying on outfits they knew they wouldn't buy, fingering the cheap fabrics with reverence for who they could become once wearing them. Margot left clothes in heaps in the corners of the dressing rooms, all off their hangers and twisted inside out. In one well-lit stall, she ignored the plastic sign that proclaimed all garments must be tried on over underwear, and pulled on a teal leopard-print thong. She strutted around the small space, a distance of two long-legged strides, in just the underwear and a beauty pageant smile. She twirled in place until she thunked down, dizzy, among the crocheted halters, denim cutoffs, and hippie skirts like white wilted flowers. She was of that special age where she knew both nothing and everything, and no matter where or at whom she looked, she saw her own reflection glimmering back like a skim of oil. She could be anyone, still.

Margot pressed the fabric hard between her legs so that some of herself remained, then peeled the underwear off and dressed, and, once outside, threw them back into the plastic bin with the rest of the animal skins—the tigers, the giraffes, the diamond-backed boas. She bought a bracelet that resembled a Slinky and a dollar lip gloss in a small, clear tube. Cupcake, it was called, and went on wet and pink. At the food court, Margot stuffed herself so that later that night, the two of them alone, she could push her mother's meal around the plate.

After she called Frankie to pick them up and Marissa went to the bathroom to pee and change her tampon, Margot leaned against the bank of pay phones and stuck her hands deep into her pockets, trying to look unbothered and attractively aloof. She knew a girl was vulnerable alone. The stolen quarters tapped against her fingers. She had two left, enough for one more call.

She inserted the coins into the slot and dialed the number she had looked up in the phone book and memorized lying on her bed one slow Saturday night. On the third ring, the wife answered, her voice like a slant of light, full of dust and gorgeous for it. "Hello?" the wife said, and Margot, as usual, said nothing, only held the phone tightly against her ear to catch the woman's breathing and imagine the blue-white beginnings of her teeth. Each tick of silence before the inevitable dial tone was almost a religious experience, confirming to Margot that she herself existed, and afterward, once she'd hung up, a soft yowling place inside of her would quiet.

* * *

The spring heat swelled and shimmered, conjuring all manner of kindred sticky things—lemonade, pine sap, swarms of early gnats. Female arachnids spread huge in the bushes, waiting for prey or for mates that might fulfill both needs. Mother and daughter caged around each other, and Frankie found herself listening in on Margot's calls: someone on Senior Yearbook Committee was "a little bitch"; the latest boyfriend was the newest ex; Margot's AP English teacher kept apple snails named for the three Musketeers; she wished she had bigger breasts and slimmer thighs; her father promised to come home soon. Information revealed itself to Frankie in slow, sure ways. But it was never the specific thing Frankie wanted to know.

In the weeks since its discovery, the note entered Frankie's consciousness while she pretended not to examine Margot, while she cooked and missed her husband's calls and as she lay in bed alone, damp against the sheets. Was that the most romantic thing a person had ever said to her daughter and had it worked itself inside of her? Had she let the boy worship? Days later, when Frankie relented and answered her husband's calls, he was sobbing, or performing it, unused to things not proceeding by his script. He said, "You should be begging me back. *You* were unfaithful," and that was true, but in the loss of herself, Frankie had time to ponder other wonders—like where had that faith funneled to and why did people deal with it so blindly? Why, following creeds of country, God, or capitalism, did no one ever bother to look beyond the words? The other man sometimes dashed across

Frankie's thoughts, important only in the way he'd made her feel. He'd been younger. Smaller than her, but able to handle her weight; he'd confessed to enjoying it. And though she hadn't slept with the man, she had liked knowing that she could. He'd taken Frankie in as she lay upon the quilt of the hotel bed as if splayed in a web, wholly pleasing to his eight eyes, unconcerned she might devour him.

Frankie wanted to caution her daughter, there were things worth more than words. Instead, she asked, "How's French going?" unable to tamp her curiosity down. Margot lifted back into her body—that temple—and flicked her eyes, and in the gesture Frankie could sense her daughter's delight. Margot *was* pleased. She knew her mother was listening at doors, and felt gratified in refusing to let her in. She said, "I'm not taking French," and battened the wall between them.

For Yearbook, Margot solicited her mother for pickups three times during the school week and every other Saturday as the year came to an end. She and nine other seniors rearranged the desks in the English classroom and brainstormed over special features and superlatives; on how to insert their own cliques into the pages as much as possible without arousing suspicion. Margot would usually have found these activities beneath her, the organization and teamwork required too taxing, but under Mr. Klein's direction, she found herself up to the task—spearheading better layouts, nixing overplayed ideas and corny catchphrases, keeping things in line. Margot liked the power of bending other kids to her will, pleased that this hadn't even been her thing but she had made it so. She liked that Mr. Klein liked it.

He was maybe in his late thirties, but well before the time he would go to seed, his angular face covered in a blond scruff that contrasted with the academic parting of his curls. He sometimes wore waistcoats to teach, dark blue and double-breasted, and Margot overheard boys calling him queer. But Mr. Klein was a romantic, a writer working on his manuscript and dreaming of Paris, the place, he'd told her, where all serious writers must go. Margot had recognized the look in him early. Knew if she wanted, she could take this, too. She started returning his gaze.

His daughter was a freshman, and sometimes hung around their yearbook meetings while she waited for her father to drive them home. The entire time, she'd sigh conspicuously and pretend to be busy playing with her Nano Baby whenever he attempted to address her. Margot enjoyed studying her, when she could, to separate Mr. Klein's features so she might understand the wife's. She wanted the daughter to like her, to want to befriend her, though she knew Mr. Klein wouldn't want it. During regular school hours, Margot sometimes lingered near the girl's locker, working up the nerve to start a conversation, and one day caught her as she vented to a friend about her mother.

"She thinks I'm too *young* to go to Prom this year, can you fucking imagine?"

"That's all they ever say!" her friend agreed.

Mr. Klein's daughter slammed her locker door. "She really is the worst. Just because she was too lame to get invited to Prom as a freshman, she wants to ruin it for me."

This made Margot feel tender toward the girl, having just been of that powerless age, and she thought, maybe this was a way in; she could commiserate, give the younger girl some hope. Margot stepped closer, clearing her throat, and both girls turned to her with their eyebrows raised. "It does get easier," Margot said, deepening her voice into what she hoped was a mature but appealing tone. "You know, with your mother—" but the look the daughter gave, one of bald disdain, cut across her before she could say anything of use.

"Do I know you?" the girl asked, and laughed with her friend, and after that, Margot refused to acknowledge the daughter. She told Marissa, sagely, you could only help those that would help themselves. Of course, Mr. Klein never spoke to Margot about his daughter directly, but whenever she was alluded to, Margot tacked on "little idiot" in her head.

After their second-to-last yearbook meeting, Mr. Klein followed the students out of the building to the place their parents would pick them up. The other kids, mostly girls, chattered nonstop, excited about their progress, Prom, and the Grad Bash trip to Disney, concerned with only high school things. He shuffled along with his hands in his pockets, dawdling, encouraging Margot to do the same. When he spoke, he directed his voice slightly up and away from her, as if conversing with the clouds. "It isn't you, calling my house?"

Margot shot him one of the looks she'd lately been reserving for Frankie. "Of course not," she said, both embarrassed and offended. "Do you think I'm a child?" The beat of silence was tight. "I wouldn't call."

"Good," he said, smiling now in a way her father might, when he thought he had convinced her that one of his ideas was actually her own. "We have to be careful." He let his hand briefly brush the curve of her hip—why did only *she* have to be careful—before clapping them together and addressing the larger group. "Excellent work today, team! At our dinner, we'll toast to all your hard work."

Frankie, parked at the curb, watched her daughter drift toward her, Margot's slender body tense, familiar in its anger. The teacher threw a hand up in greeting as they approached.

"You must be Mrs.—"

"Just Frankie, please. Nice to meet you."

"Of course! Charmed. Your daughter is a pleasure to teach, very bright." He clapped his hands again—a nervous tic, it seemed—and stepped back. "Well, good work, clochette! Don't forget, we'll meet here at 3 PM on Saturday for dinner preparations," and with that, he flashed a last smile at Frankie and bounded away.

Margot slung her bag into the backseat. "Like I don't have anything else to do with my time," she grumbled, as she climbed into the front and buckled her seat belt, but Frankie was stuck on the phrase that slid from the man's mouth, easy as a lie. She knew about the dinner; one week earlier, Margot had asked if her mother would provide a dish—*something French.*

"Clochette?" Frankie asked, and Margot was too distracted to be sarcastic.

"It means 'little bell.' He nicknames everyone in Yearbook. 'Team-building,' he says." Her daughter rolled her eyes, and with the venom of that gesture—the gravity Frankie had discerned between Margot's body and the teacher's—something awful began to tick inside of her.

"Is . . . everyone's nickname like that?" She didn't know how to ask something like this; didn't want to have to ask it.

Margot looked at her mother like she wished she'd disappear. "Mom, why would everyone's nickname be like that? It defeats the purpose." She looked out the window, toward the school, toward him. "No. That one's just for me."

The French dish and the French word. The note. Everything Frankie had wanted to know clicked alarmingly into place. And with it a luminous fury. A helplessness. She saw her daughter vanished, swallowed up by all that she could not prove.

Full up on righteousness and smoke, Frankie now steps from her car and walks up the street in the midmorning light toward the teacher's house, his door a somber blue that even she cannot love. For the moment, she is nothing but a creature of time, suspended in the motion of her body, no thought beyond the knocking.

The door opens, and Frankie must adjust her gaze. Instead of a polished wife, she finds a daughter, amber-eyed and suspicious, no older, Frankie guesses, than fourteen. Her hair is dark and shining and slick as wine. "Can I help you?" she says, though it's clear she'd rather not.

Frankie is not prepared for this. "I'm a friend of your mother's," she hears herself saying, an explanation that doesn't satisfy the girl. The daughter hesitates and then narrows her eyes, something sly glowing behind them, something a little cruel that Frankie can recognize. "She's not home," she says. "What's your name?" And Frankie, startled into honesty by the girl's authority, tells her.

"Francesca."

The girl shifts from behind the door. "Wait . . . I know who you are," she says, and Frankie is relieved that someone might tell her. "You're that girl's mother," and here her lip curls, "from the nerd club. The little pet." She tilts her head, stares Frankie head to toe. "What do you want?"

Frankie knew what she wanted, and that she couldn't have it without severe risk. She wanted to protect her daughter, who would deny, deny, deny—who would hate her; who would soon be eighteen and would leave. She wanted the teacher dead, she wanted everyone—his wife and his daughter, the whole city—to know what he'd done, and she wanted to call her own husband to tell him, finally, that her mistake had not been the affair but her inability to admit she no longer loved him.

"Oh," the daughter says. In Frankie's silence, she has come to her own conclusion, and confirmation ebbs across her face. "You're the one who calls."

"I'm sorry?"

"Don't pretend," the girl says, and Frankie understands what this daughter believes—that she is her father's distraction, French-worship in her name. The mother is out shopping with the teacher, helping him prepare for the celebration dinner—real china, sparkling cider—and they'll be back soon. "I guess you might as well come in?" She steps back, and Frankie hesitates for just a moment before she goes inside.

In the air-conditioned dimness of the living room, the girl is almost giddy, going on about all that she suspected, her features complicated by the dancing light from an aquarium in the corner of the fussy little room, cramped with dark-stained shelves, books, and brass knickknacks—the teacher's vanity, Frankie assumes.

"Are you here to tell her?" the daughter asks, and Frankie can sense that some part of the girl wants this, that she's convinced herself there must be retribution for whatever crimes mothers commit against their daughters.

"Would you want me to?"

The girl scratches her arm. Looks away. "It's better to know," she says defensively. "Maybe if she wasn't so concerned with my life, she already would." Frankie wonders if she means it, if this near-universal disdain a daughter can feel for a mother might be necessary for the appreciation that comes later, if this is what it takes to love. If she can just understand this girl, maybe she can decode her own.

Frankie inches closer—this daughter smells of green apple and rain and something slightly sour. She considers how easy it would be to let her hand fall to the girl's shoulder, let her fingers trail down the arm and trace the concave places that held those scents. It would only be fair: a biblical retribution, one daughter for another, her fingers continuing as she lays the girl back and searches out the warmth between her legs. Frankie reaches out her hand.

The phone rings, breaking the moment, and the girl's expression changes again. Now she looks wary and a little ashamed, as if she realizes that, in her resentment, she's gone too far. She tells Frankie to wait, and disappears into the adjacent room.

In her absence, Frankie recoils, catching herself on the edge of the tank, the light carving up her face. She stares into it, unseeing, at first. She feels like a monster, but what recourse does she have? If she confronts the teacher, she loses; if she doesn't, the same. But Frankie is not the teacher; she can't do the worst thing she could do, and with this realization she regains a semblance of herself. She remembers what she's good at; that sometimes, it's a mother's burden to settle.

Inside the aquarium, the teacher's snails are placid and small as plums. Now cooled, her anger suffuses her with prophecy and Frankie knows what happens next.

Margot waits outside for her mother, watching the evening disperse in bold orange and pink, a shawl of purple creeping at the edges of the sky. She's eaten, but feels an emptiness she won't learn to recognize until later as the expansion of herself—a good sign, but easy to mistake. Her mother had dropped her off at three, as planned, with two warm dishes in her arms, and she and some others helped decorate, strung up balloons and folded paper flowers into a centerpiece. She had watched Mr. Klein carry in tablecloths and cutlery, how he, brushing past his wife, leaned in and kissed the tip of her ear. The wife—attractive, as Margot had suspected—had swatted him away but was clearly pleased, and Margot found herself not jealous, but merely sad. Already too comfortable with being a phase.

During the dinner, Mr. Klein let his hand linger each time he passed a dish. The third time, Margot yanked her hand away, violently, as if burned, and the blue bowl toppled and shattered against the floor. "Not to worry," he repeated, too jovial, jumping up to grab towels. Other students scurried to snatch the roasted vegetables from the tile, but Margot didn't help them. There was no apology on her lips, and after this, the teacher made too many jokes, talked too much. He didn't touch her.

Her mother pulls up and Margot sees her first. She watches Frankie inside the car as she taps the steering wheel, adjusts the rearview so that she is peering at herself. From here, her mother looks young—could be any of the girls, making sure the face she's wearing is the one the world wants—and at this thought, Frankie suddenly breaks through, not just a mother, but a whole person. Separate and full of awe. It dawns on Margot that, old as she is, it's her mother's first time on this earth, too. Against her will, she softens.

She remembers when she used to let her mother pack her lunches, brown paper bags full of foods other kids had never heard of—endives, rambutan, tiny ramekins of fish roe to spread on pumpernickel toast. The kids, being mostly animal, were cruel at that age, intolerant of what they hadn't been taught to understand. She remembers Frankie slicing beets, fresh from the oven and steaming, their juice staining the tips of her fingers pink. *I don't want those,* she'd told her mother, though she liked them, and Frankie had asked her why. Other kids got peanut butter, cheese and deli meats, instant mashed potatoes from the lunch line. Margot said: *They look like body parts.* Frankie had set the knife down and faced her daughter. Her eyes went wide. *But they are!* she had exclaimed. *And if anyone bothers you, you tell them, "In my house, we eat the hearts of our enemies."*

When Margot thumps into the front seat, Frankie turns slightly toward her, her fingers still drumming away. "Did you have fun? Did your teacher like his special dish?" Frankie tries not to appear too eager. She'd made puff pastry filled with spinach and brie for the kids and told her daughter the smaller meal was for the teacher, a gift of gratitude. She knew the gesture would go unnoticed by her daughter, the girl inclined to think her mother always did too much. Before long, the teacher or his wife would notice the snails were missing, and the daughter would have to tell them about her visit. It would take him a moment, but then suddenly, with great horror, he'd realize what she'd done. Frankie can't help but grin at this vision; after all, what can the teacher say?

Margot refuses to talk about Mr. Klein, does not tell Frankie that he sucked the shells until his mouth had glistened. She opens the glove box and retrieves the cigarettes she's known all along have been there, her mother too sheepish to say a word. Margot takes one out and sticks it between her lips to light it, then without looking, extends it to her mother. After a pause, Frankie takes it, puts it to her own mouth. She inhales.

# Outside the Raft

That summer we were nine and ten, our birthdays rolling over one another as if playing leapfrog—first hers, then mine, five days apart. I was envious of my cousin's double digits in the same way she coveted my silver-wrapped presents, the balloons and white-frosted sheet cake, the way my parents shouted, "Happy birthday!" Except next year I would be ten, and Tweet's parents would still be locked up, serving life sentences for holding up a pawnshop and killing a man, something like Bonnie and Clyde, but no one made a movie. She lived with our grandmother, who didn't believe in birthdays and so hers passed quietly, leaving only the gift of age.

It was a typical Floridian summer, both sweltering and sweet, stretching out before us like a wide-open hand. I was giddy at the prospect of long, uninterrupted days where my cousin and I could be together. My mother never understood it, why I would want to spend all my time at my grandmother's small, slant-slatted house on the bad side of town—no cable, no PlayStation, no fresh air. What was there for two little girls to do?

I used to hear her on the phone with her friends—Toni Braxton crooning through the house on Saturday mornings, my mother decked out in sweats and an old boyfriend's T-shirt she only wore to clean in—talking about how she couldn't wait to leave Grandma's when she was a teen.

"Woman sees devils in everything," she said once, the jewels on her acrylic nails flashing as she dusted the tops of the cabinets. "Except when they're right in front of her face."

"What devils?" I asked, and she startled. She would often forget I was there, quiet, listening.

"Go play," she said, instead of answering. "Grown folks are talking." I went back to my room thinking of devils you could see—red skin, horns, and black beards. Plucked out of the pages of my grandmother's books, sitting across from you eating bologna sandwiches thick with mayonnaise. Chugging sweet tea. What did my mother think my grandmother couldn't see?

Whatever she felt about her mother, that summer she took me whenever I wanted to go. Tweet and I didn't need to leave the yard; our possibilities were endless in that small house. We spoke a secret language, and we always understood each other.

* * *

Before bed one weekend, our grandmother ran us a bath, the strawberry scent of Mr. Bubble rising with the steam. She bent over the tub, large behind bouncing, filling up our view with faded blue denim.

"Full moon," Tweet said, and we giggled over it, sticking out our own skinny rumps in poor imitation. Tweet grabbed a Magic Marker lying out of place on the sink and marked the back of Grandma's dress.

"Tweet colored on you!" I tattled, the words leaping from my mouth before I could think about them.

"No I didn't!" She whipped the marker out of sight. Our grandmother looked between us and then said, "Maybe the mark was already there," though I'd seen Tweet do it with my own eyes. After she left, Tweet pinched me in the tub, and I bore the hurt in silence as penance for my transgression. Without apology, she made me a beard of bubbles and told me I was Old Man River from the songs we learned at school.

"What am I doing?"

"Searching for your daughter," she said, then held her breath and slipped under the foamy water. And I looked and I looked, but couldn't find her because she'd turned into a fine mist floating over the sea.

In the top bunk that night, after our grandmother prayed for Jehovah to watch over us in our sleep, we stayed awake, kicking the covers off, knobby knees bumping like small rocks, our cotton underwear luminescent in the moonlight sliding through the blinds. We wondered why we weren't born as tigers roaming the green hills of India—carrying our young in our mouths, sandpaper tongues lapping blood at the kill.

"Or eagles?" My hands jumped up over my head, as if with feathers and the possibility of flight.

"Or mice," Tweet answered. I could hear her teeth chattering, and I pictured her eating cheese in tiny, hurried bites, whiskers prickling, sensing danger always. We wondered why we weren't born silver-scaled fish, instead of black girls with brown eyes and stick insect legs.

"Go to sleep in there," our grandmother called, and at the sound of her heavy footsteps in the hall we skittered back beneath the covers, holding in giggles, that soft, intimate scraping at the back of our throats. We lay together at opposite ends—long, thin feet next to heads of billowy braids and ponytails, her dark brown arm pressed against my light one. She grasped my hand in the dark, as if to check that I was still there, her nails sinking softly into my palm. "I love you, Shayla," she said.

The next day, our grandmother pulled us from our play for Bible study. We groaned and dragged our feet, made our bodies dense, hoping to be immovable, but our grandmother was a capable shepherd. She ushered us into the living room, big hands fanning us forward; we imagined wind at our backs.

"Why was Jonah punished?" she asked.

"He disobeyed God," we answered in the drawling unison of students at school. God sent a storm and the sailors tossed Jonah off their ship to calm the sea and save themselves.

"Jehovah knows your heart," she told us, giving us the eye. I thought of Jonah in the belly of the whale, his hands pressed to his lips in prayer, and what he might have said to make God spit him back up. I wouldn't let them throw me overboard, I thought, and my heart pitter-pattered a defiant beat against my birdcage chest. I had never seen a god, nor smelled one. Never tasted its sunshine flesh.

"Maybe there is no God," I told Tweet later in the backyard. The grass had shriveled and died. I threw rocks at a wasp's nest that hung from the limb of our grandmother's river birch. They missed and bounced off the papery bark, making new gouges next to scratches where the cats climbed up.

"What if He's just some big joke? To make us behave?"

I chucked another rock, and Tweet put her hand flat on my back. "Don't," she said.

I didn't know if she meant the wasps or God. I looked into her face, her large dark eyes, searching for some answer the grown-ups wouldn't give. I wanted to ask if—when she pressed her palms together before bed—she prayed for her parents' salvation or the man they killed. And to what did she pray? Did her God have two faces that looked like hers, and a gun hidden in the waistband of Its jeans? Was hers a God of pawnshop gold and two-dollar scratchers, promising *We'll be back soon*, but never coming home? Even then, I wanted to let her speak the answers into my ear like a psalm. But the subject was "grown folk talk," forbidden even between us, and so I said nothing. I threw again and missed.

Tweet wound back her arm and let her own stone fly; it found the nest with a soft *thwap* and knocked it loose. The nest hit the ground and we ran for cover as the wasps flew out, their violent droning filling the air as they searched for somewhere to place the blame. They disappeared into the unmoving sky, leaving silence in their wake.

"God's real," Tweet said, and headed for the house. She left me standing in the yard alone.

Our exchange made my skin itch, made my mind arc back to another conversation I wasn't meant to hear. My mom's best friend Shawnie had come over, and she and my mother ate crab legs in the living room, watching *Sex and the City* and trading gossip while it was off to bed for me. I was supposed to call Shawnie "Auntie," which made her own little girl my play-cousin, though I didn't enjoy Yana's company as much as Tweet's. Yana's feet smelled like toe jam and she wiggled too much in her sleep. While she snored, I listened to my mother and Shawnie talking through the door.

"How's your momma and them?" Shawnie asked, and I heard the sharp crack of a crab leg being broken between teeth.

"Girl," my mother said, like that one word told you everything you needed to know. "Too old to be raising kids again. And look how Mike turned out." Mike was Tweet's father, my mother's older brother.

"I see that same darkness in Tweet," my mother continued. "She's going the way of her parents. Bet on that."

"I don't know," Shawnie said. "I see a darkness in Shayla, too."

At the sound of my name, a deep pang quivered through my stomach, something that felt like recognition and shame. Heat spread across my face. I did a mental check of myself, my fingers and toes, my twiggy arms, the surface of my teeth. I tried to decide if my body felt evil. How could the grown-ups quantify this darkness—could Shawnie see it in my face the way some people picked out a nose like my father's, or my mother's lips? I felt for horns in my hair and finding none, put my pillow over my head. I didn't want to know what else Shawnie saw, or if my mother agreed. I tried to sleep, keeping my legs stiff so they wouldn't touch Yana's. Just in case what I had was catching.

I'd been at my grandmother's almost a week when my father came by. My mother was always talking about how cool she was even though they weren't together and he was married now. She let him see me whenever he wanted and they always did holidays together. "I don't want that boy," she'd say.

It was the hottest day of that summer and the sun hung in the air—a wax lemon melting, oozing light. "Hey, little girl," my father said, patting my head. I squinched my eyes tight and batted at his hand. His attention both embarrassed and thrilled me. I was aware, then, of my fortune, of my father there, next to me. Tweet stood nearby, and I could feel her eyes, how intensely she took us in. I shot away from him and hid my face in my grandmother's side so I wouldn't have to look at my cousin.

"We're going to the beach," my father said. "Chris and Tati, too." They were in the car outside, waiting with my stepmother.

My grandfather had been what my mother called "busy," which was supposed to explain why my father had siblings who were one year older and one year younger than me. They were bright as medallions and had soft hair like my grandmother's fake mink. Tati was the youngest and called me cousin because aunt made her feel too adult, but Chris would lord his title over me if he wanted to ride shotgun or have a longer turn on the boogie boards at the beach. The previous summer I had kissed him at my dad's apartment pool—in the deep end, angling our bodies down—six feet of chlorinated blue shimmering above our heads. When we broke apart and surfaced, Tati had cut her eyes at us. "You didn't see nothing," Chris said.

Whereas my mother kept a close eye on me, didn't want me to leave the front step, my father believed in cultivating my independence. When I was with him he'd let me ride my bike through a busy intersection to the McDonald's fifteen minutes away, or drop me off at the Wet 'n Wild water park in Orlando by myself. That summer, I hadn't seen him too much. I suspected this had something to do with my stepmother being pregnant. She'd pat her big belly and make comments like how nice it would be to *finally* be a family, like she couldn't be a family with me. She was having a boy, and sometimes I found myself wishing all that stomach was filled with air, that when it came time to push, nothing but wind would come out.

My dad handed me my green-and-black striped two-piece, my sometimes-swimsuit that lived at his house folded up in a drawer, waiting for summer. Tweet's head drooped at the prospect of my leaving.

"Can Tweet come?" I gave him and my grandmother my most winsome smile, the one that showed nearly all of my deciduous teeth, their wavy edges and baby sheen.

My dad packed us into the old station wagon, Chris and Tati scooching close to make room, and we all giggled in the backseat—like hyenas, like loons. Like children ages eight, nine, and ten. Grandma's house disappeared behind us, the cracked sidewalks and the shaggy dogs that roamed the streets. Tweet and I put the windows down and let the air whip in, sticking our hands out to fly on the breeze, eagles after all.

When we arrived at Jax Beach, my dad pulled a cooler and our inflatable raft from the beat-up back of the wagon and we piled out gracelessly, squabbling among ourselves about who could hold their breath the longest and what flavor ice cream was best. We wanted the adults to hear, to get the hint and take us to the stand-alone ice cream shop shaped like pink soft serve in a cone with sprinkles two streets over; they pretended like they didn't. We hopped from foot to foot to keep our bare soles from scorching on the blacktop of the parking lot. We complained about how hot it was: the car, the air, the ground.

Tweet didn't whine, only stood squinting into the blind sky as if divining meaning from the blue, her ratty bath towel slung around her neck. I had made her leave her water wings at home, not wanting the others to poke fun.

"Come on," I told her, and grabbed her hand, and the four of us ran ahead down the sandy paths, sunlight sliding from our shoulders, long legs carrying us carefree toward the water. We cut through the grassy pavilion where free concerts were sometimes played, past pitched cloth and plastic tarp, the homeless sheltering beneath. They scared Tweet, the way their hands darted out when they asked for our spare change. I skipped past them, unconcerned. They couldn't touch me. I trailed my laughter like a flag.

We trekked across the pavement-hot sand and picked a spot, breathed deep the warm aroma of summer—of salt and shells and seagull shit—while we waited for the adults to catch up. How slow they were, like manatees bumping along the riverbed, while we were speedboats, our turbulence gashing the water a lighter blue. When they reached us, we huffed through the setup, the laying down of towels and smearing of sunscreen onto my stepmother's back. Finally, my father brought the raft to the water's edge and we clamored in, our knees drawn up to our chins.

He pulled us out to deeper water and left us there, let the big waves push us screaming back to shore. We called to him, "Again, again!" We must have done it ten times, twenty—the white noise of roaring water in our ears—but we didn't grow tired. We laughed and laughed. A fish splashed out of the water and, far away, the thumbtack moon governed the swells from outer space. I saw my stepmother glaring from the beach blanket on land. My father saw too. He pulled us out one last time and told us we were on our own for a while, leaving to lay his head in what little lap my stepmother had left. I turned my face away from him, pretending I didn't care.

There was no big wave. The water became a vast expanse of pocked, green-tinted mirror, our plastic raft anchored on its surface. We dangled our fingers over the side, imagining they were shark bait. Our hands were blades slicing apart the water and the sky; they were telescopes spying treasures ashore that were ripe for plundering—a shovel and pail, a Barbie beach blanket. The waves we craved frolicked ahead, forgetting us.

Chris picked his boogers and Tweet had to pee.

"Let's jump out," I said. We could walk back to shore.

There was no debate. We all jumped overboard, and then we were plunging down into the ocean. We never touched the bottom. Down there the water wasn't clear or brown or green, and we couldn't see the sun.

We broke the surface, kicking, thrashing, grasping at nothing.

While we had played pirates and chopped the horizon apart, the ocean's stealthy fingers had tugged us into deeper water. It was an illusion, that stillness. Nothing ever stayed in one place. I ducked my head under the water, my eyes open and stinging, and watched three sets of small feet churning the water to boiling. Chris and I propelled our bodies down, summoning the coiled energy living in our bellies, and still, we never felt the sandy floor, though we sensed it, just out of reach. This was no apartment pool, no tame six feet. The deep here was wild, and though we could swim, there was nothing to push off from, nothing solid to direct our bodies. Tati gasped, and as if on cue, fear seized us; we became too heavy with panic to relax and float until someone noticed we were gone.

We called for help, but only the gulls heard. The raft rocked gently away, indifferent to our screaming and the salt in our mouths, the urgent pulling of currents at our toes. Up ahead, the shore gleamed bright, a tantalizing yellow ribbon.

No one came for us.

A wave rolled over our heads, and I tumbled beneath it, opening my mouth and swallowing the sea. Bright spots of light exploded beneath my eyelids, purple and blue. I was not separate from this width of water; it beat inside of me, became me. And if He sees everything, He watched us then. When I think of this moment, I imagine Jehovah peering down beneath the waves and reaching for my heart; prying it open with His dense fingers; examining my fear, the fat black rivulets spilling out. I bit my tongue and watched the blood plume before me, a small red tide in the waves. I believe it came to me, with that bite, that I was nine and beautiful and mortal. I saw us all clearly, like He would, sinking down until we were just four child-shaped stones at the bottom of the sea.

I broke the surface, the air burning a warning in my lungs, my limbs exhausted. Tati was moving toward the raft, her head disappearing beneath the water and bobbing up in jerky starts. I wanted to follow, but the raft seemed as far as the moon. Instead, I turned to Chris and scrambled up his back, pulling myself partway out of the waves, eager to escape the clutching depths. That dark, mysterious beckoning. I held onto him as if playing a game of chicken, with the fierce intent of never letting go. He threw me off, yelling, and I went back a second time, and a third, paddling toward him relentlessly, my mind bent on the word *salvation*. He flipped me from his back one last time and reeled away, swimming a ragged path behind his sister.

I had only one remaining hope—Tweet treading water next to me, her head tilted back, chin pointing shoreward like a compass, mouth sucking at the sky, too tired to scream. I clambered onto her, my nails biting into her shoulders, just hoping to float. She wasn't strong enough to throw me off. I clenched my eyes tight against her cries and tried to hold onto the world above the water.

"Get off!" she gasped, but I couldn't let go, couldn't let myself be dragged down into that darkness. I thought of Jonah sinking into the rush and how eagerly the bubbles must have broken away to surface.

I don't know how long we stayed like that, my arms around her neck. Time became nothing more than the solidity of my head above the waves. I prayed to God for someone to find us, for Him to send a whale to swallow us up. I prayed for it to be over.

That image haunts me, Tweet and me in the ocean. We never talked about it, never told anyone what I'd done. While my grandmother raises her third generation of children—a little boy and girl with Tweet's familiar features—I wonder if things could have been different for my cousin if I'd come clean about my own darkness. What if I had spilt mine onto the kitchen table where the light could reach it, let her sift through and compare it to her own? What if I'd confessed; what if my mother had stopped looking for her brother's sins in my cousin's face? Maybe Tweet could have made peace with all her loss, instead of passing it along to her children. I think, too, about the day we threw stones at wasps, when she told me God was real. I'm still shaken by her certainty. I believe that He was real for her because she'd seen His demons, and recognized them. She must've known that light could not exist without darkness; no good without evil. How might it have been if we'd told her you could be both things and still be loved? All the time, I wonder where Tweet is. What she believes in now.

Of course, we were saved that day. Chris and Tati steered the raft beside us and hauled us in. We collapsed on top of them and Tweet's shivering shook the rest of us, her panic, still electric, singeing guilt into my heart. Nobody said a word. I lay crumpled against the plastic bottom, brine pooling around my cheek, trying to pretend I was the other girl, who had not yet tasted Him. He was the burn of salt in my nose, the blue-blackness of the underside of waves.

Onshore, Tweet knelt on hands and knees as if praying to our grandmother's Jehovah, gulping air and choking on it. I sat beside her, silent, drawing circles in the sand. I didn't know how to explain myself—how I had become full of terror and light, or that I had been both the drowning and the wave. How suddenly I knew that all things must die.

I didn't know how to apologize for wanting to save my own life. I wrapped my arms around her, like a mother might, pressed my lips into her neck. Her body relaxed into mine and the shivering stalled. I heard her sigh.

"I love you," I said, and I willed the words to vibrate at a higher frequency, to jounce through her solid-seeming skin and settle in her bloodstream, as with the voice of God.

That morning there was frost on the grass. Even though Jacksonville was far enough north that this happened each year at some point—the temperature dropping to the teens, our breath, for once visible, fanning the air like bettas in their shallow pools— it never failed to shock us. There was a sense of betrayal in it. Like how dare Florida, of all places, try and turn a season.

Derrick came into the bathroom while I stood at the mirror, securing my hair with a tie. He passed behind me, reaching over my head and into the medicine cabinet, and I sucked my stomach in and pressed toward the sink so we wouldn't touch. Our reflections avoided each other's eyes.

"Be careful driving tonight," he said, spooling floss onto his finger. "News said there might be flurries."

I slicked down my baby hairs with jojoba oil and a soft-bristled toothbrush, then wanded mascara onto my lashes; I dotted blush on my cheeks. "That's good for me," I said. People got antsy during weird weather, wanted noise and bodies near them. They wanted a drink. On top of this, it was Saturday, so there was high probability I'd make bank. For this and other reasons, I was excited for the shift. I finished with my face and tidied my uniform—snapped the collar of my white, youth-size-small polo and brushed lint from my black pants. Derrick picked at his teeth, his presence large behind me, tickling at the back of my neck.

"You look pretty," he said, and, briefly, we met eyes in the mirror.

He was objectively attractive himself—thick dark hair, a large and striking nose, those arms that had made me, four years ago, fall in love with him . . . but it made my stomach drop, how little I now felt. Or how little what I did feel felt like love.

"Thanks," I said, though I didn't think he deserved my beauty. "See you later."

"Be safe."

It was a relief to leave the bathroom, our apartment, cramped as it was with all our unmet needs. Our blaming silence. We'd never called each other anything other than baby, and now, like this, it was as if we didn't have names at all.

* * *

Derrick and I had been married five months and now hadn't fucked for three of them. The last time, he'd gone soft in the middle of it and we both sat on the bed feeling terrible and too naked. This had been happening with frequency. "It's work stress. Well, stress in general," he'd said, but it still felt like a deficiency in me.

He'd initiated. I hadn't even been in the mood and now I was embarrassed. I got angry, it was hard not to, and he'd sighed. He stared at the ceiling rather than look at me, and I kept glancing at his dick, shrunken and vulnerable against his thigh.

"It's too much pressure. I get worried I won't be able to perform and won't please you or I'll make you feel bad or you'll get angry, and the more I worry, the more it happens. It's too much."

"You said it wasn't me."

"It's not. But then you make it that way."

I'd said something flip in response, as if it didn't matter to me, and he reached out one hot hand for my thigh.

"It'll pass. It doesn't mean anything about us," he said. But it did.

I thought he didn't know how to confide in people; when things were rough for him, he walled me out, and these rejections made me resistant to attempting to understand the problem. I knew my behavior wasn't helpful, but I was too caught up in being hurt by it all to meaningfully engage. Some days, I couldn't blame myself; what models did I have for unconditional love outside of TV?

After that, I started dressing in the bathroom so he wouldn't see my body, and I thought about sex constantly—the sex I wasn't having versus the sex everyone else must be. I bought a new vibrator with a soft curved tip that had eight speeds and three different undulations. Whenever I used it—when Derrick wasn't home or quietly on the couch late at night while he slept—I always came, but the orgasms were shallow, unsatisfying and quick, leaving me more frustrated, feeling like there was some deeper, better peak just beyond that wasn't within my capacity to reach. I'd felt something like that my entire life and didn't appreciate it being spelled out so physically.

I understood stress and, unlike him, could articulate mine. I was twenty-three and already starting to get nervous about so many things: aging; inhumane healthcare and the endlessness of student loans; the growing anxiety that I might not be good for much else than serving other people. I worried that we were crazy to get married so young, but was too conscious of social stigma to admit it. I felt alone. Lately, unless I drowned it out with drink and dance and work, other distractions, all day a voice way in the back of my brain, real calm, sang: Dumb girl, you'll die this way.

I pulled into the restaurant parking lot at a quarter to four but stayed in the car with the seat reclined, listening to the playlist I'd compiled for pre-shifts to force myself into a better mood. It was never a good idea to walk into a bar shift early;

you were always needed. A moment later, R.J. guided his silver Civic into the spot next to mine. I watched him through the glass as he fumbled around in his glove box, searching for something, and once he'd found it, he looked up and noticed me. He smiled and unlocked his passenger door, crooking a finger in my direction. I turned off my car and hopped out, skipping around to his passenger side, crushing my lips together to keep from smiling like a fool.

"What up playboy," I said as I got in.

"You ready to make this money, T?"

"Always."

The heat was on, warming up that smell his car had—tobacco leaves and citrus air freshener and the astringent scent of his sweat. By now I was used to it, and maybe I even liked it. R.J. leaned over the center console and hugged me, holding on for a couple of beats. He wore a big, gaudy diamond in one ear and even during shifts, I'd never seen him without a ball cap slanted backward over his short-cropped hair. He had these deep-set brown eyes, the pupils always big with whatever he was on, and a habit of licking his lips when he spoke to you, his tongue quick and furtive. Fascinating, like some kind of animal. We were friends. Prior to this, we'd worked together at a club bar called, inexplicably, Boston's before we jumped ship with one of our managers for this better-paying gig.

People often liked to say they weren't affected by other people's opinions, but I thought those people must be lying. When you heard something about someone, you were already looking through that filter, at least at first, whether you wanted to or not. So when my friend Casey had gotten me the job at the club, I asked her who she thought was interesting, and she'd said, "The barback's pretty sexy," and because of this, when I met R.J. I already had this little crush. It was nothing, not even unusual in our industry. All those tight spaces and bodies brushing throughout the night occasionally offered up moments of uncomplicated intimacy. Sometimes we'd hang out in each other's cars after close, 3 AM, just talking.

We sat together in comfortable silence, listening to the low beat of a song on the radio, the sky around us beginning to dim. I said it depressed me, the way winter stole the sun. R.J. shook the small baggie of white powder he'd been hiding in his fist. "You want?" he asked, grinning at me. He knew I'd say no, only offering because I'd been offended to learn that most of my co-workers and even the managers were doing blow on their bathroom breaks. No one had ever invited me and when I asked why, R.J. had shrugged. "You never seemed like you needed it."

"Ask me later when I'm in the weeds," I told him now, with my hand on the door.

"See you in there," he said, and winked, and though this gesture, too, meant nothing, I felt a delicious little jolt.

My regulars lined the bar, some of the newer ones I knew not by name but by their particular poisons—Seven & Seven, Bombay martini with two blue cheese-stuffed olives, Dewar's neat, the guy who only ordered what was special on tap.

Most commonly they were middle-aged, somewhat wealthy whites who liked to think of themselves as liberal, but I suspected I was the only black person with whom they regularly interacted, so surprised they were at how I was, how well they thought I spoke. I made a game of balancing my resentment of them with my appreciation; even superficially, it felt good to be adored. I laughed with my guests, picked on them—they loved to be picked on—kept their glasses full, made sure not to throw out any seasoned ice. When their food took too long, I pretended to hassle the kitchen about it, giving my patrons my "We're on the same team" spiel, all arm touches and sympathy. They never blamed me. My manager, Johnny, the slick-talking Jerseyan I'd come over with, called what we did Flirting For Money, and I was good at it. I often wondered what else my patrons saw in me. Prettiness, youth—maybe that was enough. Whatever it was, it kept them coming back, all our communal loneliness appreciating into currency.

The bar was busy, like I'd thought, the mood agitated and somehow festive. I circulated among my guests, refilling glasses, making enthusiastic small talk, slapping drink tickets down onto the soggy mat at the service well where servers waited, drumming their trays with matching frenetic energy. The low golden light of the bar bounced attractively off the large windows, fogged against the cold; made us all look lovelier than we were. I felt in my element, flushed and warm and present; there was little time to think, and I was glad to be swept up in the bustle.

Midway through the shift, the door slammed open and a chill breeze gusted in like an impatient guest. Several heads swiveled and there came that sort of hushed buzz that preceded events of interest. When the woman came into my line of vision, I understood. She was tall, blonde and blue-eyed, cloaked in a confidence which invoked inherent grace. I wouldn't have found any of those privileged, mainstream elements particularly noteworthy, but there was a smooth brownness to her skin that wouldn't be explained by a tan. The woman chose the empty stool nearest to the service well, a spot most people avoided, wariness sparking off her like cold-weather static. My other patrons watched her with doggish intensity as she shrugged from her calf-length coat and sat. She grabbed a menu and plainly ignored them, and I wanted to applaud.

I set a napkin down in front of her. "Hey, welcome. I'm Trinity," I said, my standard greeting. "What can I get you started with?"

She looked into my face, traces of cold still lingering, pink nose, wet eyes. She was stunning. "As in the Father, the Son, and the Holy Ghost?"

I laughed. "I don't think so. My mom just liked the sound." She ordered a scotch and water, and after I brought it to her, I asked her for her name. She leaned over the bar toward me, a smirk playing around her mouth. A perfume of jasmine and rose escaped the collar of her shirt.

"Are you ready for this?"

"I'm ready."

"It's *Snow*. I'm not shitting you. Can you believe they named me that?" She sat back with pride, as if this were her favorite thing about herself, her success with producing incredulous reactions in strangers. I wondered if this forwardness was a defense mechanism, and if I had something like it too.

"Hardly," I said, deciding to indulge her, and she showed me her ID. She looked several years younger in the photo—blue and blonde there too. I raised an eyebrow and started making a ticket of Don Julio margaritas, extra salt on the rim. "Wow, your parents were really on one."

She tucked her ID back into her wallet and took a deep pull from her drink. "Aren't you going to ask?"

"Ask what?" I said, though I knew she knew I was playing dumb.

Snow sucked her teeth, then fluffed out her hair and pointed to her eyes. "It's all real."

I held up my hands. "You don't have to convince me," I said, and though I'd checked for dark roots, I never would have asked. Mostly, I was just an ear, letting my guests tell me what they wanted to, offering in return what complemented their stories, or propelled them. They wanted to talk about themselves, and always the wildest things. I was a sounding board, some kind of budget therapist. The more I let them talk, the more money I made.

Snow told me she was Vietnamese on her father's side and that people, no surprise, constantly fetishized her. My gut leapt in recognition. "They just come right up to you and ask, 'What are you?'"

"Or if they're polite," I added, "they say, 'Where are you from?'"

Snow was a touchy-feely type, like me, easy to talk to. She leaned forward, held my eyes when she spoke. I filled up my other patrons' drinks, got them extra napkins and au jus, whatever they needed, but I could feel her, a gleaming at the corner of my vision, and I kept ending up right back in front of her.

Eventually, Snow told me her father had recently died and because she wasn't close to him, she felt a weird sort of grief. "A car crash. He got in an accident on 95 and a semi hit him. He saw it coming." I made noises of condolence, but I could tell that wasn't what she was here for. I could identify her kind a mile off—whatever she was going through, she just needed to name it.

Jemma came to pick up her margaritas.

"You like that upsell?" she asked me, arranging the drinks on her tray.

"You know I do." The higher the bill, the better my tip out.

Jemma said she was having a party at her place after the shift—no, a *get-together*. Just a few of us from work, some colored bulbs in the lamps and a living room full of bass. She said, "Come," and the command made me shiver. I told her I'd think on it. Something broke in the kitchen and several people at the bar thrust their drinks into the air and cheered, "Opa!"

Snow asked for another scotch, then started up again like her father was on both our minds.

"I think I've been dreaming about him," she told me, pressing the glass to her forehead. The condensation wet a streak down her face. "I wake up in the night with this bright terror." She told me that one night recently, while sleeping in the unfamiliar house of a new lover, she'd again woken up with the feeling and gotten up to pee, fumbling in the dark. She'd run into the closed bathroom door while flipping on the light. "It was this, like, simultaneous interaction. I'm not sure which happened first." She said there was a mirror on the front of the door, and when the light came on, for just a millisecond, she hadn't recognized herself. Snow sucked on the ice from her glass. "I saw what my face would look like if I died in surprise and fear. What my father's face must have looked like. There's nothing scarier than that." She said she started seeing a hypnotist.

"I don't know if I believe in that," I said, plopping a garnish-cherry into my mouth. I didn't even like them, sugary as they were, it was just something to do, but as I worked it in my cheek I became hyper-aware of Snow watching. I swallowed.

"So you don't believe in star charts? Or like *energy*?"

I stacked dirty glasses at the sink. "I don't know. It all just feels too . . . whimsical. Or immaterial? Too much like coincidence."

Snow nodded, the way we do when we doubt what someone else has said. She told me, "By the end of the night, I'll convince you." I just smiled in response; I thought I understood her. Deep in the mire of grief, who didn't seek companions?

The ticket machine spat up an order of four strawberry daiquiris and I groaned. Real drinkers—people who sat at the bar—never bothered me with frozen drinks, but the main diners, with their penchant for fruity or flashy, could weed you quick. R.J. sauntered over, a languorous grin on his face, doing to me what we did to the patrons, working me, turning me soft.

"Sorry," he said, touching my hand, and I couldn't be too mad. He was the one who got me ice when I was low, who went back into the kitchens to check on my orders when most other servers claimed they didn't have the time. We had an arrangement: I made all of his drinks first.

"Don't let it happen again," I said, and poured mix into the blender.

He leaned on the bar while I made his ticket, eyed Snow the way everyone had been all night. Then he said to me, "You in love?"

I made a face. "What are you talking about?"

R.J. inclined his head at Snow. "You've been staring all night." I started to deny this, but stopped when I realized what it meant about me—that I could be both a victim and a perpetrator of gaze. I ducked the implication, saying, "So, what, you've been watching *me*?"

I considered that this was all being human amounted to, layer upon layer of looking.

R.J. laughed. "If you're ready for that break, get Johnny to cover the bar." He loaded the drinks onto his tray, the daiquiris already starting to melt under their own weight, and hustled back onto the floor. Maybe I did believe in energy—his body left a signature. A trail I could almost follow.

"That your husband?" Snow asked, and I startled. Everything that was wrong between Derrick and me came rushing back. I twisted the white-gold band around my finger. Often, working the bar made me feel inscrutable, anonymous, but with Snow peering at me under her lashes like that, the idea seemed ridiculous. I was a fish in a bowl, and if I was analyzing my customers, some of them were doing it right back.

"My husband doesn't work here," I said shortly, and turned to run fresh water in the triple sink. I was annoyed. I didn't like thinking of Derrick in this space. It was too easy to pit him up against some simpler ideal, and it made me feel unfaithful. I thought about how we lay in bed at night, our stone bodies breathing in the dark; how only inches separated us—his dreams and my wakefulness—but it was that growing metaphysical distance that felt impossible to cross.

This sudden awareness of myself clamped over me like a lid. I did a quick sweep of the bar and then called for Johnny. "Take over for a minute? Seat two's waiting on a plate of fish-and-chips."

"Be quick," Johnny said, and he slid into the work, second-natured. I watched him surreptitiously tip a bottle over his Styrofoam cup, then dried my hands on a towel and left the familiar tumult of the bar for the kitchens, its food-slick floors and different, harsher light. The din of plates sliding into the window, metal clanging against the grill, the line cooks surrounded by steam and swears, as well as laughter. It was like passing from one world into another—the acceptable order the guests could see, and the chaos that made it possible.

R.J. sat in the usual smoking spot, around the side of the building near the enclosed dumpsters, out of sight of patron view. The cooks had drug out three old crates for chairs and a table. R.J. nodded at me as I approached. I sat next to him and wrapped my arms around myself. Our breath garlanded the air.

"You going to Jemma's party?"

"Are you?" I asked.

R.J. brought out the baggie and it seemed like half the coke was gone. He scooped some out and took a hit, thumbing his nose against the burn.

"I might. If you go. I have more fun when you're around," he said, then reached over to tug gently on my ear. The spot glowed with warmth and traveled through me, striking hard between my legs. My body felt made of stars. I admitted to myself, right then, that what was between R.J. and me was maybe not nothing. Easily, I could imagine him as a lover, and what that quick pink tongue would do.

The hugeness of R.J.'s pupils seemed to suck at me, and finally I had to turn away.

"It's cold," I said. "We should both get back in there."

"Here, warm up." He measured a bit of powder onto the back of his hand and held it up to me. I looked from him to his hand. There were only two more hours in the shift, and the high was so brief. Who could it hurt, other than myself?

The hit landed right between my eyes, making them water, and R.J. smiled, like he was proud of me. He said, "Now we can finish strong." The drug came on almost instantly, shuddering the cold out of my body. My heart pumped faster and little tremors zipped through me, a kind of focus. I could taste it in the back of my throat.

When I emerged from the kitchens, Johnny was looking in my direction. He pointed to his wrist and threw his hands up, and I held up one finger and ducked into the ladies' room. He'd be snippy about it, but I needed a moment alone. The restroom was mercifully empty, and I braced myself against the sink, the star-feeling throbbing on and off. If I went to Jemma's, something would happen, and as bad as that would be, I knew it was the easier option, a ready-made out. Harder was facing that I was too impatient or lazy to understand the work of love; behind that, my glowing fear, my almost certainty, that I wasn't worth the effort. I studied my reflection and found it difficult to look into my own eyes; like Snow, I couldn't recognize myself.

The door wooshed open and she strode in, like I'd summoned her.

"I saw you come in," Snow said. She pulled a vial of liquid from her purse and held it up for my inspection. I was already shaking my head when she asked, "Want to try something?"

"I've got to get back to the bar," I said. I kept feeling like someone would walk in and bust me for every single sin, and if it happened, I'd deserve it.

"It'll take just a second." She crossed to one of the stalls, her bright hair whipping behind her, and leaned against the frame. "You don't believe, so you've got nothing to lose."

"What is it?"

"Holy water from the mountains."

I wasn't certain why, but I walked toward her and went in. We fit inside the stall facing one another, our backs pressed against the thin walls, the toilet between us. The slender space, dim lighting, our solemn eyes—all of a confessional mood. I dared her to convince me.

Snow sprinkled the vial over my head, then lifted both hands and passed them in front of my body like a scanner, slowing at critical points, my third eye and throat, hovering over my belly button and lower. She said, "You're going to have problems with your chest."

I blinked. A pressure ticked at the base of my skull. "What do you mean? Like physically or emotionally?"

"You know what? I don't really know."

I laughed, not bothering to hide my derision. I put my hand on the latch, eager to return to the bar, that golden light, where I knew how to manage. "Well, thanks for that," I said generously, and as I opened the door to leave, Snow said, very quiet, as if talking to herself, "I don't know why you doubt he loves you."

Spooked and hopeful, I looked over my shoulder at Snow but quickly rearranged my face. "I don't know what you're talking about," I lied, and left the stall, pushing through the main dining room and back behind the bar.

Johnny scolded me, lovingly, and I tried to drop into the work, refilling, wiping down, teasing, but I could feel sweat gathering under my arms, my heart racing. I told myself it was the coke. Snow came back out, and I could feel her trying to catch my eye. I flitted from customer to customer, laughing too loudly, trying to drown her presence out. I swooped up an empty pilsner, foam clinging to the side, and it slid from my grip, shattering at my feet. "OPA!" my patrons roared, as if they'd been waiting for this, and in the upset, I finally looked at her. Snow stood up and put on her coat, all of us watching. She set her empty glass on the money she'd thrown down, and once she was gone, I slid the damp bills from the bar top and counted them—a 50 percent tip. Then, like a sarcastic fairy godmother, Johnny appeared, handing me the broom so I could clean up my mess.

After the shift, my high worn down, my co-workers loitered in the parking lot, stripping to undershirts, passing around body spray and breath mints. R.J. paced near our cars, his hands in his pockets. It didn't feel as good as it used to, to know he was waiting for me. He gestured to the others hyping themselves up for the party. "You coming?"

"Um," I said, opening my door, "give me a sec." I sat behind the wheel, pretending to check my makeup in the rearview, buying time, and R.J. leaned down and said into my ear, "Don't worry. You're pretty," before leaving to join the rest. I stared after him, the emptiness of his words touching down in me. I wanted to go home.

I could see him so clearly, my husband, as I hadn't been able to for months—tired, off from work, wrestling the trash from the can. He tied it up carefully and hauled it to our front door, forgetting his jacket, flipping on the hall light so that when I came home I would not stumble in the dark. The flurries promised flickered through the night like restless spirits, the flakes so delicate they would melt long before their cold could reach him. I watched him drag the bag to the curb and pause. Maybe he looked at the moon, full and ringed with frost, or maybe he looked for me.

# Necessary Bodies

Management didn't remove the glass bottles, burger wrappers, used condoms, or the cigarette butts—they just dyed the water blue, a kind of golf-course aquamarine Billie had to squint and step closer to make sure of as it frothed from the fountain that ran from nine to nine. Even standing there a few minutes, she couldn't tell if the hue was only a trick of light. The women in the front office were dreadful, a sneering bunch who had lost their charm as soon as she and Liam signed the lease, so she stopped the first maintenance guy she saw as she crossed the parking lot, one with whom she was on nodding terms. It was an easy relationship that required no names. She said, "Did y'all color the pond?"

"Looks good, right?" he said cheerfully, his white-white teeth flashing in the sun as he hauled cardboard boxes into the back of his utility vehicle. "You can't even tell it's not real."

"Mmm," Billie said, inclining her car keys toward him. About as real as those veneers, she wanted to say. Everyone knew Jacksonville water to be mostly brown. Moss swayed lightly from the oaks, suggesting breeze, but if there was one, it was a dead wind and even the sidewalk seemed to sweat. A heron ducked its gray head under the ripples, plucking something up and swallowing it—a small fish or maybe a piece of plastic, confused by its glint. She wondered if the pond now had a new taste, a smell or texture that, as humans, they were dumb to. There were turtles in that retention pond, ducks, minnows by the hundreds, and at least two giant carp that patrolled the shallows, smoky-scaled and silent until startled, opening their mouths to green algae and miniature ecosystems tumbling in. What would the dye do to them? She refrained from voicing this as well; there was no time for a debate. As usual, unluckily, she was late. She wished the maintenance guy a good day and got into her car where she thumbed a text to her mother—who more than likely was already seated, peering over her menu toward the door, constructing a slick reprimand for her daughter: *I'm otw.* Her mother replied: *I was so hungry I ordered an appetizer! See you soon!*

Billie waded through the dining room chatter, the business types on lunch hour gulping down sweet teas and giant salads smothered in ranch, noodle-armed women leaning over the table talking urgently with their friends while their children made toys of the sugar caddies. Servers weaved in and out of the jumble laden with trays but nimble, in flow with the rush. Her mother was seated at a booth for two, picking daintily at a platter of fried cheese. She looked beautiful as always—hair freshly relaxed and swept from her forehead, a black shift dress, her legs smooth with shea butter.

"Last night I dreamt of fish," Colette said, even before her daughter could sit. For a moment, Billie couldn't separate this statement from her earlier concern, wondering how her mother could know about what her complex had done to the pond in the interest of rental value. But then the moment passed and she had to work hard to control the grimace pinching at the corners of her mouth. "You know what that means," her mother continued, and unfortunately Billie did. That old wives' tale. Colette meant fish as in fertility, as in birth and babies. *Grandbabies.* "Last time it was cousin Em. Maybe this time it's you?"

"I'm on my period," Billie lied, tossing a glob of cheese into her mouth. It was the quickest way to get her mother to stop, although the pass only ever lasted until the next month.

"It doesn't have to mean *right now.*" Her coy mouth, an irritated flick of her wrist. "It's prophecy. I haven't been wrong yet. And you know, if you really wanted to do something for me, that'd be the best birthday present. I'm ready to be a Mimi." Not Nana or Meemaw and certainly not Grandma. Colette didn't look old enough to be anyone's grandmother, she commonly remarked, and she wanted to keep it that way.

In two Saturdays it would be her fiftieth birthday, and this was the reason Billie had dragged herself up from a late-night stupor to be with her mother. She was acting as the chief party planner, assisted remotely by her younger sister Violet. At thirteen, Billie had asked their mother why she'd named them the way she had. Old-fashioned, a boy and a flower, leaving her children open for schoolyard mockery. *Billie Violet,* Colette had said, used to ignoring her daughter's moods, *doesn't that just sound like some kind of special? Like that jazz singer's name?* Billie never asked why her mother squashed the names together, as if she and her sister were one person, instead of two.

"So, you just always wanted to be a mother?" Billie asked finally, knowing she couldn't get away from the topic without at least a little discussion.

"Yes, of course. You'll come around to it. You'll see."

That easy assurance, almost arrogant. Like the coloring of the pond, Billie couldn't tell about this either, whether her mother's view was a slow truth or patriarchy. Was it that simple? Somehow she didn't think so. Colette had her young and single, and Billie remembered clearly her mother lying on the couch some days after work, the room darkening around her, their apartment always two steps away from tidy. How she kept a hand over her eyes and even in stillness seemed tired, like it took great effort to be in her body. When Billie misbehaved, Colette would say: *I put food in your mouth and clothes on your back,* as if Billie had come to her mother in spiritual form and begged her to be a parent.

Billie remembered how once when she was ten, early morning, her mother had gone to run an errand and left her and the infant Violet sleeping in her bed, the baby surrounded by pillows. As far as Billie was aware, neither of them had moved an inch the entire time their mother was gone, except as soon as Colette returned and opened the front door, Violet turned on her side, right off the bed. Violet's cries came raw and walloping, punching through Billie's sleep. She remembered her mother, panicked, rushing into the room and grabbing the baby up from the hardwood. The scowl she'd tossed her way. And later, still angry, Colette had leaned down in her face, her voice expansive as heat, and said, utterly calm, *I love you, but sometimes I don't like you at all.* She wondered if her mother remembered and where all of this fit into coming around.

Their server came and they ordered—salmon for Colette, who claimed she was watching her figure, the grease of the cheese still on her lips; a burger for Billie, who was not, but felt more and more pressingly that she should the further away from twenty-five she got. Her mother made so many modifications to her meal that by the end, she had ordered off-menu, so Billie kept hers simple, smiling broadly at their girl as she whisked away their menus, hoping to convey that they were good for the tip; somehow no matter where they went or how they acted, their behavior or appearance, their being, was always under scrutiny.

Having said her piece, Colette moved on. She said Violet would get into town late Friday night before the party and would crash on Billie's couch if Billie was willing. This wasn't a problem. There had never been any real animosity between the sisters, so far in age as they were, no grudges from their childhood. They were half-siblings who never thought of themselves that way; they liked each other, even if they didn't talk all that often, the two of them comfortable together and apart.

"I want midnight margaritas! Dancing music! Gold balloons, gold everywhere!" One of her mother's friends, male and moneyed, was footing the bill, his present. Colette wanted a pecan-studded red velvet cake, a rooftop, White Party prominence. She wanted, in her own words, flash and pizazz, to be seen—attention kindred to that which she'd commanded in her younger days. A mood like the omnipotent buzzing around a honeycomb. "Are you writing this down?"

Billie pointed to her temple. "Mind like a steel trap," she said, and her mother speared a hunk of fish at the end of her fork and brandished it in her daughter's direction. "Yeah, okay. And when I blow out my candles, just know what I'll be wishing for."

Maybe that was part of the problem, Billie reflected as she stuck her key into her apartment door; that this was how it all felt—like someone else had made a wish and sunk a penny down into the deep of her. She tossed the doggie bag of leftover burger onto the counter and tripped into the bedroom, where Liam and the puppy were still snuggled in the covers. She let her body drop onto the sliver of unoccupied bed. She wished she could still fall asleep like a child, like a husband.

Liam turned toward her, cowlicky and sleep-soft, reaching for her reflexively, pulling her into his large warmth. The puppy repositioned himself between them.

"You're going to be late," Billie murmured into Liam's neck.

"I'm getting up," he said, making no move to do so. She and Liam saw each other mostly nights and weekends: she was freelance, working from home while he managed the twilight hours at a major shipping warehouse Monday through Friday. He left around two, got back most nights after midnight or later. Most of the time she would wait up for him, and when he came home they ate dinner together or she drowsed with her feet in his lap while he watched shows to unwind. It was far from perfect, but they made it work.

"You didn't tell her did you?" Liam asked, and Billie laughed so viciously it panged hard in her sternum, like a fist. "Are you kidding?" she said. "Who do you think I am?"

Billie liked their marriage, the humor of it that sustained when it was easy, and when it wasn't. Even when she was dark, Liam really got her. For example, when they'd first got the puppy, a yippy small thing, she'd said, "If the zombie apocalypse ever happens in our lifetime, we'll have to kill the dog." And immediately, he'd answered, "Only if we eat him. Waste not, want not." She loved that about Liam, that she didn't have to censor herself or worry that he'd think she was bad. Sometimes she despised her husband, but in that way you could only achieve with someone you'd lived with for a long time and deeply loved. She appreciated that they could talk about the hard things. That they could admit the hard things were sometimes funny. However, she hadn't yet been able to ask him what the zombie policy would be on the baby. That news was still too fresh to joke.

Three days ago the doctor had put her at six weeks and no one knew except Liam and her best friend, Pia. Maybe the dog. Billie didn't feel bad about lying to Colette. It would have been too much on top of everything—her mother's proprietary joy, an unequivocal testament to her own deity. Plus, they didn't know if they would keep it. Billie tickled under the puppy's chin until he was rowdy and pouncing and biting the tip of her husband's ear. "All right, all right," Liam groaned, rolling over. "I'm up."

Once Liam had shit and shaved and brushed his teeth, he came back into the bedroom to talk to her while he pulled on his work pants, buckled his belt.

"What've you got going on today?"

Billie still lay sprawled across the covers, the puppy wriggling happily into her armpit. "Besides existential dread? I'm working on a piece for *Harper's*. Something like Pluto's demoted planetary status and how it equates to the revocation of female autonomy."

"Hmm, sounds super related." Billie threw a pillow at him and Liam bomb-rushed the bed, landing lightly on top of her. "I'm serious! I could see it. I mean, you know us men. Indian givers, right?"

"Don't use that term, white man," she said, smoothing down his hair. "They deserve much better than y'all."

He held up two fingers, Scout's honor. "It is henceforth stricken," he promised, then took those same fingers and slipped them under the rim of her jeans, down down until he'd struck the center of her own heat, finding an easy side-to-side rhythm. He was so familiar, so good at it. Billie pushed the dog off the bed and closed her eyes, unbuttoned her jeans to give him more freedom. Lifted her hips. Almost let her conscious self fall away. Then the glimmer of what was newly between them. She pulled his hand up and kissed him in a way that was also a shove, the gentlest of rebukes. "Isn't this how all the trouble started?"

She fastened her jeans and followed Liam to the door. "Try not to worry too much," he said, jamming on his shoes. "Whatever happens, I'm right here with you." And Billie knew that, and appreciated him saying it, but the cold fact of it was, this was a fear that truly only resided with her—*within* her— a hitch in waiting, cellular and primal. She thought how much simpler it would have been to be the giver, Y chromosomed, to have lived up to the implication of her name.

After he was gone, Billie allowed herself a half hour of wallowing, of composing checks and balances, yeses and noes, while she scrolled idly on her phone, but the news was awful and she had work to do. She vomited casually into the toilet, then took the puppy for a short walk around the deranged pond and put him in his crate. She texted Pia: *Have to do research. You down to ride?* Pia, consistent since their college days, responded within ten minutes: *I'm free. Scoop me up.* She ended the text with three eggplant emojis, so Billie knew she was serious.

* * *

They bought tickets at the Museum of Science and History, paid a little extra for a four o'clock interactive showing at the planetarium on celestial bodies featuring black holes. It was a quiet time to be there, an adult time, since most kids were sitting at kitchen tables with English workbooks and pre-dinner snacks. Other than a handful of others—some old folks consulting pamphlets and a group of teens with a perpetual look of indifference stretched between them—they practically had the place to themselves. All those whirling lights, hidden compartments, displays of ancient bones. All of the discovery.

"This girl at work said the best thing about being pregnant was that her boyfriend didn't want to fuck her because he was scared of hurting the baby, so she got to grow her bush fully out. She hadn't seen her herself like that, like *ever*, and said after the itching phase, she really enjoyed it."

The blonde woman at the counter, who had not welcomed them when they entered as she'd done for the previous guests, threw them a scandalized look, but Pia only waved.

"Do you believe that?" Billie asked.

"What, that she liked it?"

"That he was scared of hurting the baby."

"Not for a second."

Billie wondered, if they kept it, if Liam would still want to. He told her all the time that he would want to make love to her even when she was eighty, but she thought that was an easy thing to say when old age never felt like it would happen, not to them, not directly, not yet. Billie still used celebrities' crow's feet as a measurement of how much physical time had passed—she was just starting to be able to see age in herself. Maybe the transformations of time and pregnancy on the body were related. If she asked him about sex, Liam would say of course, but once he saw that alien belly, the skin pulled shiny with some other creature's being, he might change his mind.

They walked through the exhibits, and Billie was relieved to find them safely distracting: aquatic life, regional birds of prey and the required dinosaurs, a hundred-year history of Jacksonville starting in the 1800s: Cow Ford, the Great Fire of 1901 (though a noticeable skimming of the city's part in aiding the Confederacy). There was nothing to remind or sway her. No genome projects or working models of the human heart. But Pia must have been waiting for a chance to extrapolate. They'd just ducked inside an oversized circuit board, the wires and glow bouncing off the walls, when she said, "Okay, so let's chart this thing out." Each item she ticked off on her fingers like elementary math: Billie and Liam had been married five years; they loved each other; they were in their late twenties; they weren't broke; they liked other people's kids; and both their families got along. "It looks good on paper, right? How do you feel? What are you thinking?" She was really asking, not being patronizing or waiting to inject her own opinion, and this made Pia all the lovelier, her dark eyes collecting the generated light, and Billie tiny there, suspended upside down.

She was thinking a million things, some of which had plagued her even before she'd found out: What if the state floods; we reelect that terrible man; if I'm bad at it; I do it and then decide I don't want to do it; if I don't do it and miss it; what if someone shoots me in the grocery store, the movie theater, my own home; what about the revisionist histories taught in schools; what if I'm not self-sacrificing enough; if I'm *too* self-sacrificing; if me and Liam get divorced, shit happens; what if the kid hates me; if I'm cruel; if I really really love it and lose it; if none of this can be sustained, not our love or our planet? What if, in the end, we just dye the ocean and wish it well?

For better or worse, she didn't know if it was responsible to bring new life into this world, but she couldn't spend all her time agonizing. She had to keep moving, keep breathing, or else she'd cease to exist, so she gave Pia the simplest of answers, what it could all boil down to: "Honestly? What will this baby do to me?"

The planetarium seats reclined all the way back so that each occupant had an expansive view of the ceiling, and at 4 PM exactly, the lamps went out and the room transformed into the nebulous black of the universe—their own solar system and thousands upon thousands of stars blinking awake, many for which, amazingly, overwhelmingly, there still were not names. In that dark and intermittent light, Billie was a seed, a blip of yearning in the deep pocket of the galaxy, small in the most comforting of ways. The ubiquitous male voice-over gave a brief tour of each of the eight planets, poor Pluto, the asteroid belt, before moving beyond, to the closest black hole, three-thousand light-years away from the Earth. They learned specific terms: *space-time, event horizon, ideal black bodies*—that last made both women independently chuckle—all used to interpret a mass so large that even light could not escape it. Once an object dropped inside, it was essentially lost to any external observation. However, it seemed to Billie that in this instance "lost to observation" was not mutually exclusive with "gone." She leaned over and whispered into Pia's ear, "Do you think a black hole is a portal?"

And Pia, after only a moment, replied, "Life's a circle, you know? You can't go anywhere someone else wasn't first."

"So what have we got so far for the diva's big day?" While still on the line, Billie texted her sister all of the details, sent her pictures—the rooftops she'd scouted, the plastic gold-rimmed flutes—and Violet volunteered her opinions, what she agreed with and, citing her "relevant youth" (Billie inferred this as style), what she thought could be improved. She said her midterms were murder and she was dating this guy, and she still hadn't found a suitable gift for Colette. The sisters prepared for Violet's arrival, hashed out the last particularities that would need to be attended to the day of the party—Billie would pick up the cake from the shop in the mall and her sister would decorate the venue. "And *please,* honestly, y'all are so *old,* but if you and Liam get any ideas to bump and grind while I'm there, just give me a heads-up."

Billie could hear the exaggerated shiver in Violet's voice and she asked her sister if she had any real perception of age, if her sister knew of the theory of time accumulation, which illustrated that the more one acquired, the faster it seemed to pass. Billie asked these things snootily, as if she had not just recently learned them herself. "Not yet," Violet said, laughing, and they got off the phone.

Billie told Liam what her sister had said when he came home that night and he laughed to himself as he called the puppy and leashed him. "She does know we've had sex all over that couch, right?"

Billie assumed not—it was her understanding that people tried to imagine as little as possible about other people's lives unless it suited them.

While writing her article, she took breaks from researching intersectional feminism and the baby moons of Pluto to Google water shading and its effects on aquatic plants and animals. Most sites claimed the color was food grade, and therefore safe for the animals and for the human consumption of those animals; that it prevented the spread of certain undesirable algae and the poaching of valuable spawning game by predator birds—*a win for everyone*. But Billie wasn't fooled; she knew that, worldwide, money was the cult over all things, no goodness or sin excluded. She was witnessing, in her news feeds and with her own eyes, how much a life was worth. Late at night, while waiting for Liam, Billie searched random things:

"how many years FL underwater" and "when will the sun go out"; intergenerational trauma and its biological effects; an article in the *Florida Times* where they interviewed the grand dragon of the local chapter of the Ku Klux Klan about his renewed recruitment efforts while sipping sweet tea in his home; how to make homemade, organic pizza rolls; why the term *cocksucker* bestowed disrespect only on the person performing the action but not the possessor of the cock.

Certain of her own complicity, Billie got into the habit of picking up stray litter in the parking lot. Every day she checked for dead carp.

In the last slice of Friday, Billie picked Violet up from the airport. Her sister's body was springy, new-formed and golden in her crop top, the boyfriend-cut jeans. She'd fastened silver cuffs to her baby locs and wore rings—jade and onyx and amethyst—on each of her fingers. Violet, somehow, was taller than Billie and more confident than she'd been at twenty. The entire ride home they didn't speak of themselves, and instead cranked the radio loud and scream-sang early Kanye, Maroon 5, and Avril Lavigne, the era of pop that coincided with the short stint they had occupied Colette's house together as minors. The sky ahead of the road was streaked purple and felt a little like driving into nothing, made them feel immaterial and a little spooky, like maybe "self" was a myth.

Billie's phone rang, just as she expected, and she answered the call on Bluetooth. "You got my baby?" Colette asked, and Violet mewed hello into the speaker. The dashboard clock flicked to midnight and both sisters, as if planned, shouted, "Happy birthday, Mom!" They could hear Colette crowing, clapping for herself. Their mother said, "Thank you, babies! Praise Him. Now both my girls in one place. Now I can finally sleep," and Billie wanted to ask if motherhood was always that way—waiting for rest to find you, for parts of yourself to come back together.

Billie made a pallet on the couch and shook a pillow into a clean case. She hadn't meant to tell her sister anything, but the news came out, slippery, into the drowsy quiet between them. Violet sucked in a breath. "So it's you. Mom's been grilling me for weeks about safe sex, about the importance of *finishing my education*. I been trying to tell her I don't ever miss a pill. How'd she react? She throw a parade?"

Billie turned her back, folded down the sheets. "I haven't told her yet."

"Ohhh, waiting for the party. That's smart. You're going to blow my little gift out of the water." She made a drum of the coffee table. "Daughter of the Year goes to . . ."

"It's not like that."

"Then what's it like?" Violet asked, and Billie told her. Her sister's face scrunched into an expression that managed to demonstrate both confusion and displeasure. "So you're, what, afraid the baby's going to 'disrupt your life'? Isn't that kind of selfish?"

How to tell her sister—a baby herself, they both were—that this was the easy claim, citing the cities you had yet to see, the career you had not yet made. Telling yourself there was time later, of course there was time. Kids could be irritating, and even the most basic scars no longer faded entirely from her skin. Billie knew this baby would wreck her. How to convey that all these reasons could be true, were valid, but that there was another monster lurking behind disruption, a logic that told you that motherhood was not just some rite of passage, another stone to put in your pocket. That this would be a whole person, one you would be responsible for keeping that way, and what if you ruined it? Surely, not everyone was meant to be a mother—not in this conventional sense—and what would the world be now if women had been allowed more freedom to wonder?

"Look, don't tell Mom. I need to figure this out."

Violet took her small bag into the bathroom, the toilet flushed, the sink ran, and she came out some minutes later in sweats, face shiny with oil, and her hair secured with a satin scarf.

"I won't say anything. It's not my news to tell." Violet got under the covers. She kept her eyes on Billie. "But maybe you could spend one day as if you *were* going to keep it. Maybe quit calling it an 'it'? I know you don't think I know anything, but what if it's worth a try?"

"Fake it 'til you make it?" Billie said, trying to joke. She ducked low and kissed Violet's cheek. Violet smiled, and there was a gravity to it, like something else was looking out from underneath her sister's young face, ageless and terrifying. A truth.

"Yeah, why not? You think anyone really knows what they're doing?" Billie couldn't remember, when she was Violet's age, if she'd been so ignorant and wise.

In bed, the puppy cuddled against Billie until Liam came home to take his place. She felt him tuck in beside her, the scent of shower water still clinging to his skin. She pretended to be in deep sleep, somewhere far away, her body a void. A space worthy of nurturing; worthy of love, and when she finally dropped down below consciousness, she didn't dream. Or if she did, this, too, was above her understanding.

The cake was not ready—thirty more minutes the bakery promised (they had previously promised noon)—so Billie had time to kill. Violet was already at the venue with the box of decorations: streamers and tablecloths, the flutes and gold balloons. Pia would meet her sister to help, then take them back to the apartment where she and Violet and Liam would dress to Colette's specifications—in spangled blue or black or silver, like old Hollywood money or their closest cocktail impressions of such. Billie's dress—one-shouldered and mermaid pearlescent—hung neatly in the car, and after picking up the cake, she would drive to Colette's to get ready.

While she waited, she wandered around the other areas of the department store, browsing the aisles of beauty and home improvement, the sad rows of tanks holding dim, limp-finned fish. All these things one could buy whose promises, at best, were half-full. She found herself in clothing. First Women's, Misses, Children, and then, unavoidably, Infants. She'd, perhaps, been heading there all along. Everything on the plastic hangers was tiny, soft under her fingers, pastel and color-coded into two conditioned genders. While she was trying to imagine what was developing inside her buttoned up into a fox onesie complete with hood and furry ears, she felt a presence behind her.

"Billie the Kid?" An old high school nickname she had first hated, then grown into.

She turned to find a man—a low fade to hide his thinning hair, a tiny gut falling gently against his polo. His face was familiar but she was blank to his name. And then, in a warm and sudden wash, he came to her. Freshman year, a popular boy she'd briefly liked and had never had a chance with—Quentin, a sophomore at the time. She shook her head at her luck. Jacksonville was so wastefully big that only rarely did she run into people she used to know, and never when she looked this good. "Q?"

"Well shit, it *is* you," Quentin said, a sleepy smile breaking over his face. Some of his old charm sparkled there. He stepped forward and wrapped her in the kind of hug people gave when overtaken by nostalgia, that made friends of even those they'd only barely known. Billie let herself be folded up and hugged him back, pretending too. "How've you been?

You shopping for yourself up here?" As he released her, she closed her eyes. Paused in the small quiet. She leaned into her sister's advice.

"Actually . . . yeah. My first child." She beamed. Placed one hand over her stomach like she'd seen so many women do, this universal signal. "We're so excited."

"That's dope! Congrats! I've got two myself. When are you due?"

And because she owed him nothing, Billie found she could speak freely, and everything she had not voiced, all the good that could come from this, burbled up from the deep. She spoke effortlessly: the spring due date, possible names honoring grandmothers or great uncles, how she and Liam would wait until birth to discover the sex, they didn't want to put pressure on an outcome. She told him, with manufactured relief, that holidays and weekends would *mean* something again. Quentin agreed this was true, asked her if she had one of those baby tracker apps—his girlfriend had been crazy about hers. He congratulated Billie again. "It's a miracle, truly. I mean, don't get me wrong, you'll be tired as hell. But I just learned so much about myself. You just gotta hang in there."

Billie wondered if it was possible not to sound like a motivational speaker when making small talk with those you'd casually shared a history. It was amusing but also a little nice, being this magnanimously positive. It was harder with people who knew you better. She and Quentin parted ways with another hug, empty assurances that they would keep in touch—but the thing was, she *was* hanging on. To this image, this baby as real and fixed in her life, her hands still cupping the small mound of herself. She could sense it as she hadn't been able to before, more than just a wave of nausea, a needling thought. Violet had been right; visualization was key.

She saw a soft cheek, open to touch, and the reassurance of someone needing you. Someone you would come to need right back. She saw her mother's pride. The company of three. That she would be changed. Billie pictured herself serpentine—lean and sleek. Circling around until her lips touched her own belly, and she could press them against the flesh that had gone firm and hot as a stone left in the sun. She saw her mouth whispering into the baby's ear-buds, into that secret space between them, the words umbilical, passing through flesh and water and finding land: *I love you*, she was saying, *but sometimes, I don't like you at all.*

Colette was glowing, leaning against the outside bar with a cocktail in her hand, telling a loud story, the only figure in all that sparkle clothed in gold, as she'd planned. It was a good turnout, her friends old and new, her family, and even Billie and Violet's fathers had deigned to come, dressed in suits, Billie's father wearing a blue porkpie hat with a new penny tucked in the brim. After their daughters had greeted and left them, the men stood bunched in one corner of the rooftop, sipping dark liquor and talking furtively, as if they hadn't been invited and didn't want to call attention to themselves.

Both sisters found this comical. "What do you think they're talking about?" Pia asked. "Trading secrets about your mom?"

Colette had come up behind them and she worked herself between her daughters, snorting into her glass. "What those two got to say, other than what a good mother I am? And how lucky they were to ever get a taste?" Then she strode toward the men, waving as she came, like a queen. Their fathers looked diminished and bashful in her presence. Pia cackled while the sisters lovingly rolled their eyes. Liam, his glass near empty, shook his head.

"Your mom is a capital T trip." He rattled his bitten ice. "I'm going to the bar. You want anything?" he asked Billie, and then blanched at the sudden stillness in each of the women, that common question now loaded with weight. "I mean, any of you," Liam clarified. Billie cleared her throat. She'd been sipping glasses of seltzer all night, each time garnished with fruit to throw Colette off the trail. But she liked drinking, especially at parties. She liked the buzz and giddiness and the lightness of her body as the alcohol suffused her bloodstream, as she lost herself to music and movement on the dance floor, beyond the point of any past or future—only present.

"Well, I'm not of age," Violet said, though Billie had no doubt her sister indulged, would do so now, while their mother was optimally distracted, if not trying to make a point. Her sister's face was a map, and Billie could see where any affirmation on her part would lead.

She shook her head. "I'm good for now."

"I'll have whatever you're having," Pia said, and Liam shuffled quickly away. Violet made some excuse—that she was going to check on the hors d'oeuvres, request a song—and disappeared, leaving her judgements behind her.

"I see you told her," Pia said, her eyes trailing after Billie's sister.

"It slipped out."

"Do you think she'll tell your mom?"

Billie sipped from her glass, straining seltzer through her teeth. "I'd wring her neck and she knows it."

They stood quietly, their thoughts eaten up by the party, all those people. Billie watched her mother flit from group to group, watched her dance, her dress sparking light onto whoever was near. Liam returned with the drinks and leaned close to Billie, the heat of rum on his breath, his lips cool against her ear. "Let's dance," he said. "Forget everything for a little while." He led her to the floor and they crashed through the pulsing bodies to the center, and Billie threw her hands up, directed her feet and hips and shoulders in seamless rhythm. She obeyed.

Just before midnight, well after "Happy Birthday" and the cake, a couple of servers rotated through the remaining guests, offering trays of margaritas prettied-up with starfruit and lime. The grand finale. Colette's send-off to the first day of her fiftieth year. She stood before them and toasted, to her great fortune—her daughters, her friends; to her long life and fifty more years just like the last. "What I've learned is, you've got to live. And you've got to be grateful. Don't entertain regrets! And don't let no man run you!" Everyone cheered—the men somewhat reservedly—and drank to her, to the promise they saw for themselves.

Billie stood at the back of the crowd, near the double doors that led inside the restaurant, where servers moved in and out, breaking down the last of the food from the party and returning abandoned dishes to the kitchens. She was alone. A server passed by with a spare drink on his tray and Billie found herself reaching for it. The glass was slick as an eel against her palm. She looked around, fingering salt from the rim. No one was watching, no one who would care. Billie tilted the glass to her mouth, inviting the cold rush against her teeth, the tang and salt. Even watered-down, the tequila was clear in the mixture, a brightness. A bite. She finished it quickly and set the empty glass on another passing tray. Her hand went up to her mouth, where the chill still lingered, the taste. One drink, she told herself, couldn't possibly hurt, and even Colette had preached *No regrets.*

Of course, as soon as she thought it, the idea became real in opposition. A panic seized her. Billie threw herself into the restroom, into one of the stalls, and knelt down on the sticky floor. She thrust two fingers at the back of her throat and gagged until her eyes watered and burned, but couldn't bring the drink back up. "Sorry," she mumbled, hiccupping into the bowl, but she knew that it was only a word, that it excused nothing.

Billie wished she were home so she could crawl into bed, clothes and makeup still on, and sleep thought away. She wished someone else could make the decision. That someone else would say it. She was wiping her mouth with a square of toilet paper when she heard the clacking of heels. The stall door nudged open, her mother's anxious face hovering there. Somehow she'd known, alerted by some motherly sense. Arriving, as always, even mistakenly, at the source of the trouble. Colette had on the same look she'd worn when Violet had fallen, before she'd been able to judge the harm that had been done and marched into the safer territory of rage. But here, between them now, there would only be comfort, no guilt to force her mother's hand. Colette bent over Billie and rubbed her back and Billie thought, maybe even anger was a kind of love.

"It's okay, baby," Colette murmured, clucking. "You just had a little too much. Go on home. Drink some water. Tomorrow's another day."

The streetlamp on their side of the pond was out when they pulled up. Liam cut the engine and looked over at Billie, who sat staring ahead, seeing nothing. Violet had wanted to stay at Colette's for the night and Pia, graciously, volunteered to drive the two of them home. Billie hadn't told her husband what had happened, but he saw the smudged mascara, sensed her interior mood. He knew her well enough. He touched her hand and only then did she open the door to step out. The heat had cooled in the night, leaving the air tepid as a bath.

"You go up," she told Liam. "Get the dog."

He jingled the keys, wary, but then he agreed. "I'll be right back down."

After he retreated, Billie turned toward the water. Now the pond was sky-colored, glassy and dark as a universe. Minnow mouths opened and closed, puckering the surface like rain, and even so, with the fountain switched off, the water became a mirror. Revealing. Something to skip through; to be lost in or found. Billie considered that maybe anything could be a portal—a black hole, a body, a choice—and elsewhere, unobservable, every turn not taken continued on: there was a Billie who crafted songs instead of stories; one who lived a single life in Seoul tutoring English; another parallel to this current one, beckoned in the dark by nightmares, by that maternal sense, a glass of warm milk in her hand. An infinite number of almost-Billies, not lost, but just out of reach on the other side. Wasn't it possible that somewhere, a child called her by another name? That, though she couldn't see them, the carp were still swimming? Billie closed her eyes. She felt the night pulse around her, dark matter talking back to the matter of her.

Behind her, footsteps. The puppy barked—one short, deliberate yip. Recognizing her. Hailing her as his own.

# Thicker Than Water

Our mother calls at nearly midnight, well past her usual sleeping time, so I know something has a hold on her. Some bug or a ghost, sleepless itself and unrelenting. Me, I always was a creature of night.

Enough, she says as soon as I answer. You and your brother will make peace. You will spread your father's ashes in Santa Fe. Like he wished.

I pick at a pimple nestled in the folds of my left armpit. It appeared sometime during the course of the day, among the in-growns, painful, not yet ready to burst. When I withdraw my fingers, they are damp and smell lightly of onion. I wipe them on my shirt.

What about work, Mamá? I ask, when work—my mutable employment as a dog walker and babysitter—would never be the issue.

Just a couple of days. You can make the time. I can see what she looks like over the phone lines, the scarf covering her graying curls, her face determined, sheathed in darkness; how her words are a prayer but also a bondage. Cecelia, she says, it's been too long. Your father needs rest. But what she means is, we all do.

After we hang up, I sit a moment holding my phone in both my hands. The flicker from the TV blues the room, accompanied by a nostalgic heaviness. My brother is of night, like me. For the last year, I have avoided thinking of him, across town, separate in his wakefulness. But our mother has summoned us, and there is no escaping that call. I dial. He answers on the second ring and this tells me he's been waiting for me, as I've waited for him.

Lucas, I say. His name feels unfamiliar in my mouth, a little sour, but with a honey to it; I haven't said it in so long. Mamá just called. He sighs and it sounds like storm.

I know, he says, and my silence concedes my utter secondness—in this news as in the order of our birth. Of course she called him first. I wasn't the child who needed convincing.

So? Are we doing this?

Two weeks from now. I can take four days, no more.

Our mother wants us to drive. To really see the land, she said—the red hills and the cacti standing tall as soldiers—but we both know she wants us to share a small space. To have no other option but to mend. I sense every reluctance in my brother, his petulance clear, seeming stronger than even those days when we were little and hassled one another over every inch of ground, and I can't help but prod, he being a natural extension of myself.

Still a smug little sister, I tell him, We'll take your car.

When Lucas turns up in the driveway of our grandparents' old house, where I live alone, he honks like a bad date. He hates coming inside, to this place where our father had lived as a boy after our grandparents moved him from his beloved Santa Fe to Tallahassee. Nothing similar in the two places, our father often said, but the vigor of the sun. Sometimes I, too, felt our father's presence in the halls—a figure standing distantly, unmoving, one hand raised toward me, as if in toast.

I appraise my brother through the windshield in the early morning light, my travel bag slant against my hip. In the time since I've last seen him, he's grown a beard and shorn the waves of his head into a close fade and, because he is vain, everything is kempt. Through the glass, his face is apprehensive, as if cornered, and there's something I long for in that guarded look. He is lovely. I had set my hair in braids the night before and this morning let them loose around my chin, then put on extra-strength deodorant and foundation for the purple blooming beneath my eyes. I want to appear beautiful to him and without guilt, like someone who's been wronged but can contemplate forgiveness.

Lucas speaks first, sticking his head out the window. You getting in or what? He pops the trunk and I throw my bag in next to his and slide into the passenger seat and it's like old times, except everything has changed. An orange light glows on the dashboard. CHECK ENGINE. And I say, pointing to it, Do you think we'll make it?

Our mother opens the door even before we knock. She's packed us lunches in brown paper bags—ham and Kraft cheese sandwiches and two tangerines each. She seems relieved to see us there together in her living room, even awkwardly, unspeaking, our bodies angled away from one another. Our pictures are everywhere, clearly dusted and attended to; us as kids, us as a family before fracture—evidence we'd started somewhere and sometimes it was good. Lucas turns his face from it.

We can't stay, Ma. We've got a lot of road to cover, he says, because he senses, as I do, that she wants us to linger in this past. He kisses her cheek to dull the rejection.

I understand, she says, and hands the lunches to my brother. Then she turns and places our father carefully into my arms, the ceramic urn taped closed and wrapped in one of her good scarves. White linen with a pattern of peach dahlias, the bundle no bigger than a newborn child. She crosses herself, mumbling blessings into the air, and unlike Lucas, I can't kiss this away. Cannot turn my face. This is Arlo, our father, and he is everywhere in me. He taught me how to cook, how to type, how, when walking, not to look down at my feet. He had always been precise with me and did not treat me as a child. He told me the names of things; when there was death he called it death, and when he tucked me in at night he would say into my ear, Por la sangre, and wouldn't leave until I repeated it back. Until I made him believe that I believed it. I had loved him and was frightened of him, as he thought all good daughters should be.

Leaving, our father at my feet, Lucas turns the wrong way down the road.

Freeway's the other direction, I say.

He rolls his eyes. We've got one more stop to make, he says; then, Hold on to that, speaking of the urn. I don't respond, but bracket the bundle better between my sandals. An image rises up: the lid coming undone and our father's remains pluming into the car, coming to settle among the lost pens, crumbs, and parking stubs. How we would look stopping at the nearest gas station, covered in him, how reverently we might scrub our faces in the restroom sink. One of us would insert a quarter into the coin-operated vacuum and funnel our father away while the other leaned against the car, crunching a handful of BBQ Fritos. Arlo, in the end, just one more big bad dust bunny. I laugh out loud, and Lucas shoots me a look like I've lost it. Maybe I have.

We pull up to a bungalow, painted sage, with a screened-in front porch and tie-dye mandala sheets for blinds. On the porch I see an old patchwork couch, a lazy ceiling fan. There are books stacked on a milk crate at one end and a philodendron in a clay pot trailing its leaves through the speckled light. Lucas gets out and I realize his intention is to go inside. I realize he *lives* here, in this different place I do not know.

I thought we were pressed for time, I say.

He's already climbing from the car. He says, You can wait here if you want.

But I'm curious. I follow him up the short concrete stairs, through the porch—it smells like rosemary and weed—and into the house. The living room is small but surprisingly homey. It feels airy, full of ease and light. Lucas disappears down a hallway and I gaze around at the charming secondhand furniture, the framed Dalí poster propped against a wall. I don't recognize anything as my brother's until I see his turntable and records strewn across the breakfast bar. I feel a small pinch of relief, which quickly vanishes as an orange sherbert cat hops down from the TV stand to investigate, curling her small-boned body around my ankles. He hated cats.

That's Lucy. I look up to see a silver-haired white girl leaning against the wall of the hallway where Lucas had gone, and now everything makes more sense—the plant, the books, the cat. This co-op vibe. I should have known. When the girl moves into a patch of sun, I can see the curve of her cheek is faintly furred. In the light, her hair becomes lavender.

Oh, I say, and not wanting to appear startled or rude, I ask if the cat is named for Lucille Ball, that iconic redhead. She says, No, named for the devil for her wickedness. I'm Shelby.

I tell her my name; that it's so good to meet her, when really what's good is that my brother brought me here, let me come in. A promising sign on our horizon. I'm making a note to tell him that I appreciate this—once we're on the road, some miles between us and the strangers we've become—when Lucas appears again. A purple duffel stamped with heart-eye emojis dangles from his hand. I look from his face to the bag. From the bag to the girl. Sorry, she tells me with a crooked-toothed smile. I was supposed to be waiting outside.

They leave a key under a loose floorboard so their friend can feed the cat. Shelby moves toward the front passenger seat and I can tell it's not out of spite, but habit. Automatic shotgun. Girlfriend privilege. I stand close to Lucas as he situates her bag in the trunk and turn my face so there's little chance my lips can be read.

This isn't what Mamá meant, I say, stoking the displeasure in my voice, and he bends lower into the trunk. You wanted to take my car, Lucas says. My car, my rules. And I can't argue with that. These laws are nonnegotiable. When we're all buckled up and the engine is running, Shelby swivels and presents our father's urn to me, like she's offering a treaty. The mood between us feels that sacred.

My condolences, she says, and I take him. After a moment I put our father in the seat next to me and buckle him in, too, so that every time Lucas checks his mirror for the road, he'll have no choice but to see.

* * *

Shelby doesn't believe in evasion, which I find out when I tell her how lucky it was she could get the time off work for this trip and ask her what she does. We're on I-10, driving west through the panhandle. Out the window, unremarkable stretches of field.

I'm a foot fetish model, she says, and I gawp at her rosy little toes, her feet propped up on Lucas's dash, old smudges on the windshield from past contact like abstract art. Her nails are painted a vivid, acid green, which is not her usual color. Her clients like French tips and hot tamale red. She tells me she had a friend who had a cousin who got her started, but after she blew up, she got her own site. Shelby breaks down the specifics of her job—the brand of pantyhose her clients prefer, level of packages she offers; how much people pay for nothing more than watching her stroke Lucy's fur against her high arches. She explains the smelly feet trope.

Like, you know, I've just gotten back from a looooong run, and gosh, my feet are sooo tired, so sweaty, and then I make a big production of taking off my runners and my socks and all that. I can't tell you how many socks I sell. She says she does some of the normal shit too—lace and leather, oh baby I'm so hot for you, just with more feet.

It's great, she says, nodding. It pays the rent and I can set my own hours. Plus all the cute shoes and pedis I want. You know, people will buy stuff off your Amazon wish list.

I try to catch my brother's eye in the rearview, to see what he thinks about all of this, but he's resolutely not looking in my direction. I can't tell anything from the side of his face, but his right hand hasn't moved from Shelby's thigh. What do you do? she asks, and I say, Basically clean up shit for a living. Play with people's human and fur babies. And she says, That's awesome, like she means it, and I find myself liking her for my brother.

By hour two of the drive, she's turned around in her seat, talking exclusively to me, as Lucas hasn't felt the need to participate. I appreciate her attention, which keeps me from feeling like a child in the backseat. It turns out that Shelby is also a purveyor of random knowledge—interesting facts she collects off Wikipedia and Reddit chat rooms. She knows about wine-making, the chemical makeup of methamphetamine, what the stars of the *Real World: Key West* are up to now, and about the golden-age architecture of Roman Catholic churches. Shelby says, So, I'm sure you've heard about all life originating in Africa, but have you thought about what that means? That, like, the first gods were black too?

I can tell she's wanted to ask me this probably since we'd met. She wants me to know that she's an ally. That for her, my brother is not a fetish. She wants me to be impressed. I want to tell her that she doesn't have to try so hard—Lucas and I both grew up exoticized in a mostly white school system, so this is far from our first white-partner rodeo. I want to recount all the ridiculous things we've heard over the years as proof of allyship—the black best friends and A-pluses earned in Spanish Lit—but she's been nice to me, so I humor her. I tell her, borrowing from Hurston, gods often reflect the people who create them. She doesn't catch the reference. I ask her more about herself, tell her what I've been up to lately, as if we're old friends catching up. I'm speaking to her, but I imagine her as a medium between Lucas and me, what I hope he has missed coming through a messenger he's more willing to receive.

The three of us have steel bladders, so it's a while before we stop. When we cross into Mississippi, we pull into a dingy gas station off the highway just outside Lucedale. None of us have ever heard of the chain. We all get out to grab snacks and stretch our legs. Shelby and I walk to the restroom while Lucas pays for gas at the counter. The cashier's eyes flick over us, cowboy mustache bristling. He doesn't speak, only takes my brother's money. Once in the stall, squatting over the discolored seat, my curiosity is finally stronger than my repulsion, and I ask Shelby through the wall: Did you meet my brother off the foot site?

Oh no, Shelby says, laughing. I can hear her wiping, flushing. I never meet clients in real life. They met at Floyd's, a college club on the Strip where one of my brother's friends was deejaying, and started dating just before our father died. She tells me sometimes Lucas appears in her videos, faceless, doing things to her or letting them happen to him. I don't ask her any more questions, and speak just so she'll stop. Lucas was never the jealous type, I tell her, which is true except when it concerned the affections of our father. While we're washing our hands with the diluted scentless soap, Shelby asks, What about you? Seeing anyone special?

Define special, I say, trying to sound light. My foundation is holding up and my hair still looks great. Maybe she'll think I'm a cool shoot-from-the-hip, love-them-and-leave-them kind of girl. I haven't had a serious relationship since before our father got sick. And even then, I didn't like to lay myself out that way. Love requires a bareness, a certain pliability, and I didn't thrill at the possibility of being transformed or wiped away. I look at myself in the mirror but instead see Arlo's tired face—the drawn, long pull of it after he and our mother fought. The two of us are in the living room alone, late afternoon, the light amber in my hair while I play dolls at his feet. I am six and happy, and he clutches my chin and tells me, If I could, I'd marry you.

Shelby lowers her voice conspiratorially.

Okay, so here's a tip. Attraction is all about chemicals. We're just like animals, you know? She explains that humans secrete pheromones in urine and in sweat, and even if we're not aware of it, our bodies react. So, she says, what I do is get that clean sweat after a light workout, spritz a little essential oil, but leave my original musk. Here, smell. She beckons me closer and lifts her arm, and to my own amazement I lean into her smooth white pit. Under citrus I detect a smell that's a cross between chlorine and celery. Not welcome, but maybe not unpleasant either.

And that's how I got your brother. She winks at me and flips her thin hair, which moves and shines as if liquid.

I'll keep that in mind, I tell her. I wish I could unknow everything she's said, but her sharing has given us allegiance to one another. As we walk out, she threads her arm through mine and I let her.

Back in the car, my brother cranks the AC and gives Shelby a look.

You took long enough. I thought that clerk was going to shoot me.

Sorry, babe, Shelby says, and pops the top on a can of seltzer. She offers him a swig, which he takes, then she reaches into the lunch our mother packed and grabs a tangerine. Once peeled and quartered, she guides a slice between Lucas's lips and the bright juice bursts across his chin. Shelby wipes it away and absentmindedly licks her finger afterward, and I look out the window because such lazy intimacy is too much to bear. You want one of these sandwiches? Shelby asks me like they're hers to give, but I don't respond. I'm too busy wondering what it's like to be so comfortable in your own body, you don't try to mask the scents of its functioning but instead make a profit off them.

I was always fearful of my own smells—of how they condemned or conspired against me. Our mother instilled in me early what evils might come sniffing, though she never illuminated the specifics. In her stories, they were hungry shadows who preyed on incautious girls. What I knew, I'd learned from our father. *National Geographic*, two lions roaring onscreen, the male biting the lioness's neck. Arlo pointing, his dry voice in my ear: They're having sex. It looked painful. Scary. Bad. This was the evil our mother meant.

I see myself, fourteen, fifteen, in the bathroom, perched on the closed toilet. My underwear is a tangle around my ankles and in the cotton seat, a teaspoon of off-white glop. Sometimes it had a shimmer like pearl, and when I brought it to my nose, it smelled of egg or nothing at all. A boy at school had just begun reciprocating my clumsy flirtations, and I needed to know if any of this was normal. I call for my mother to join me, and when she enters, I can't look her in the eye. Already I know that what is between my legs is a hunchbacked sinner, a thing to hide, but I stand and face her, offering my underwear in one hand and parting myself with the other.

Does this look okay?

Our mother curls her lip, but even then I didn't think she meant it.

It's fine, she says, and leaves immediately, not wanting to perform the double work of shaming me, since I've already shamed myself.

Lucas insists on driving the entire first leg and pushes our half-and-half schedule an extra hour. The day is a blur outside the window, meaningless, the sky eventually reddening until it bleeds itself a dusty orange. Shelby finally talks herself out by the time we reach Texas and now snores in the front seat. I like it this way; I can better interpret my brother's silence, which shifts and deepens like music as the hours tick by. It feels less hostile and more unsure, like a space I can slip inside.

Around nine we find a Motel 6 on the outskirts of Dallas and Lucas rents two next-door rooms. When he returns, he leans over Shelby in the front seat and says something into her ear, nudging her gently until she wakes, a shy, satisfied grin on her face. We carry our things inside, which for me includes our father. The rooms are typically dank and eerie, but we weren't expecting much. I place the urn next to the ancient box TV.

I'm starving, Shelby says when we regroup outside. We all are. We had split our mother's sandwiches and the rest of the tangerines hours ago. There's a burger joint across the street, so we order doubles and triples, extra-large fries, even shakes, like we're celebrating. We take everything back to the hood of Lucas's car and eat together under a wink of yellow moon. Lucas and I sit on a concrete parking block and he rolls a blunt from weed they'd hidden in a coffee can and my heart unfurls. My brother is soft when he's high.

White Grape? I say, pointing to the rolling papers. Those had been our favorites.

What else is there?

He licks the blunt and lights it, and after getting it started, hands it to me. The first hit rolls through my body clean as wind, and I hold it as long as I'm able. When I exhale the sweet musk, the night opens above us, wild and listening. We smoke the joint small. Everything is better—the burgers, the shitty motel. Ourselves. I look at Shelby, sitting cross-legged on the hood like an ornament or a seer, the way her pale belly folds over the denim waistband of her shorts. There's no shame in her. She smiles at me, then inclines her head toward my brother, inviting me to make a move.

I say, Remember that time you told me sugar ants were sweet? And I ate some?

Lucas sniggers, his body loosening with the laugh.

You were such a dumb little kid, he says, smiling. Ma was so mad.

Our father had been madder, his expression grave at the sight of my swollen mouth. He'd kissed my forehead before pulling his leather belt from its loops in search of my brother. I don't remind Lucas of this.

He says, Remember Abuela used to call us both pequeño chucho for years and we thought it was just a pet name, until the Mexican cousins told us it meant we weren't pure? And you cried!

We both cried, I say. But then we pretended to be dogs that Easter. Howling and lifting our legs on the furniture. Remember everyone thought it was so funny except Abuela? Mamá said we hurt her feelings.

Remember. Remember. Remember. The black moccasin in the community pool. The P.E. teacher's false eyebrows. Lena Crosby and her pink glitter thong. This part is easy, time breaking open to slurp us smoothly into the simpler past. Where Lucas and I had bitten and scratched and punched and kicked and tricked and teased each other and still we went to sleep side by side. Shelby listens, her presence gentle as a chicken's egg.

Lucas is still laughing about the last thing we remembered when I say, Do you remember the year he put the presents on the roof? Because we forgot to leave the window open for Santa? We had no chimney and our father warned us that if we forgot, Santa would skip our house. Lucas goes quiet and I press him. Remember? We woke up and started crying because the tree was bare but then he climbed up on the roof and there they all were in a plastic sack? We believed in Santa that year. My brother says nothing.

Remember he used to sing to Mamá on the porch after dinner? And at bedtime he sang us to sleep?

He only sang when he was sorry.

No, because he loved us.

You and I remember things differently, Lucas says, and I'm offended that he thinks memory would work any other way.

But you remember "por la sangre," I say, dangling the words before him like tainted bait. Lucas spikes his burger wrapper to the asphalt and an ugly part of me hopes he remembers how he failed, and that it haunts him.

What's it mean? Shelby's question darts between us, a startled neon fish.

Basically, blood is thicker than water, I tell her, but I'm still looking at Lucas, whose face is tilted to the stars.

Shelby scratches a scab on her ankle and her voice hitches an octave. There are speculations, she says, that that's a misquote. That actually the phrase might be: The blood of the covenant is thicker than the water of the womb, which would have the opposite connotation than how it's commonly used. She says that in Arabic lore it gets even stranger. They say, Blood is thicker than milk.

But neither of us is listening to her. My brother is leaning away and I'm now on my feet. I can feel my eyes glittering, a tight fury around my body, black as that pool snake. I had wanted to spin him one more memory, something good that could ease this hurt—but my tongue feels bitten. I say the wrong thing.

Remember what he looked like in the hospital the last time you saw him? Lucas stands too and the night shrinks down until it traps us. We aren't touching, but I can feel his body shaking and, like a bat, I use this to pinpoint my own location. I feel blurry and grateful—how much love it takes to hate this much.

I remember, Lucas says in a low, dangerous voice, and we broadcast the memory between us: our father attached to all those tubes and Lucas leaving, refusing to speak. Lucas, a perfect match. I run after him down the too-bright hall and grab his arm; I swing him toward me and his hand is balled into a fist. I clutch him. Please do this, I beg, please. It's a scene, some bad TV-movie, but no one blinks an eye. This is normal here. People surge around us as if they are river and we are desperate stones. Please, I say. Por la sangre. And Lucas looks at me, and behind his quiet rage lurks an unmistakable pity. He asks me, After everything, how can you believe in that? and I have to barricade him from my life to keep from knowing the answer.

Come on, we're all tired, Shelby says, and now she's the one tugging my brother's arm. Our moment breaks and I know tonight I won't get what I wanted. Shelby collects our trash into a grease-stained bag and they turn to go. Our father taught me to swim, to play dominoes, how to pop the meat from a crab claw. Our father is waiting in my room.

What did he teach you? I call out after my brother and he actually stops. Lucas looks at me, says, How not to be a man.

In my room, listening to the soft sounds of them on the other side of the wall, I conjure the memory that would have saved us: Lucas and I small, before our parents cut his hair. We are snarls of black curls and big dark eyes. We are doppelgängers, genderless, whole. We wrap a sheet around our shoulders and climb into the kitchen cabinet, where we pretend we are unborn, and we have always been together.

In the morning, I take the first shift. Lucas slouches in the passenger seat with his hand over his eyes like he's hungover and Shelby sits in the back with our father between her thighs. Finally, there is desert and the sky is a blue wonder against the barren mouth of the road. Our silence feels complete here. We stop for packaged pastries, weak coffee, some gas. We drive. We stop to pee or to pretend to, just for one moment alone. We drive. We say nothing. We almost burst from saying so much nothing.

We're on the 40, just past Wildorado, when Shelby lurches forward between the seats, her finger an arrow at the glass. Look out! she cries. I jerk the wheel to the right and swerve hard around whatever is in the road. We bump onto the shoulder and something pops, the car lurching, breaks grinding, and we slide on the sand before we stop, dust feathering around us.

What the fuck! Lucas says the same time I do. I take the key from the ignition. We get out to check the damage.

Shelby says sadly, It was a coyote.

Lucas squats at the front right tire and even before I ask, I know that was the pop.

Jesus Christ, he says, his hands on top of his head.

Why didn't you check this before we left? I ask him, my mind spinning to the orange light on the dash. He says, This had nothing to do with me. You *hit* something.

I cut a glance at Shelby. I wouldn't have if I wasn't trying to avoid hitting something *already dead* in the road.

Shelby says, I'm sorry! at the same time Lucas growls, Don't get started on her.

Fine, whatever, I say. Let's put on the spare and get out of here. Already the sun is baking us, wanting to strip us to our basest selves. There's sweat in my hairline and on my upper lip. Today I am not beautiful.

I don't have a spare, Lucas mutters.

What? Who travels without a spare! I yell, and now we're squaring up, face-to-face and close to touching. Almost.

I'm just doing this for Ma. I didn't want to be out here in the first place! he tells me.

If it weren't for you, maybe we wouldn't have to be.

This spawns the kind of quiet that gathers lightning. Lucas leans in even closer and whispers, Not all of us pretend to forget. Just because you can't face what he did, what you let him do to you—

I strike his face, and when I do it, I mean it. The sting of the blow warms my palm and spreads, jubilant, through my body. This physical connection, however violent, is what I've been waiting for. What I've missed.

Shelby pushes between us, as if to protect us from each other, but when she stands facing me, her arms outstretched, I understand exactly what she's standing between and where her lines are drawn. Y'all cool off, she commands, all her wispiness evaporated. My brother and I are winded, both shocked, and I know my contact translates differently in our separate skin. Lucas swats the air.

Forget this shit. You wanna go to Santa Fe? I'll drop you at the bus station.

Shelby tells him to stop it. She checks her cell phone, then his. No service, she says. She takes deep, yogic breaths. If she suggests I do this too, I know I'll lose it, but instead she says she and Lucas will walk back to Wildorado. We're not too far past. She tells me to stay with the car. Lucas and I neither agree nor disagree, but I fling open the car door and stretch sullenly across the backseat. Shelby digs through the glove box and tosses something into my lap. A switchblade. She says, Just in case, and they go.

Hot and exhausted, I stare at the sagging roof, blinking back despair, and now I'm with our father, the lions rutting in the tawny grass. The lights are off in the bedroom, so the creatures blaze. I am six and the dark is a jaw around me. In the shadows, our father transforms. He's only Arlo, and his close, adult musk overwhelms me. They're having sex, Arlo tells me, his hand a dry heat on my belly, and when he says it, something I don't have language for enfolds me like a womb. His hand is still and conscious, with its own heartbeat, and I'm a good daughter—loving him and afraid. I am as still as his hand, but the dark swallows me all the same.

I claw up and out of this memory, back into the car where, at least, there's light and Arlo is only ash. Only father.

I know Lucas is bluffing. That Shelby will talk him down. They'll come back with the tire and we'll go on. We'll honor our parents' wishes. But I imagine myself rising, exiting the car and opening the urn, the small puff of dust like a constricted cough. I imagine fishing through the fine silt of our father, snatching a hunk of bone and laying it on my tongue, the muscle flinching at his grit, and while he's still between my teeth, tipping the urn and letting him go to roam this lonesome road with the other restless things.

I shift against the backseat, skin sticking to the vinyl, careful not to upset the urn. My shirt is damp under the arms now, two dark patches growing like eyes and I can smell myself. Root vegetable. Earth. A murkiness. I try to sink down into the depths of my own scent, try to linger, to like it. But it's too intimate and I'm an animal of habit. I jolt up, scrabbling for fast-food napkins in the center console so I can blot away the stink. Out the window, Shelby and Lucas are specks converging on the horizon, at that particular distance where it's hard to tell if someone is walking toward you or away.

# Exotics

Among themselves, the members called it the Supper Club; to us it was only our J-O-B, and no one, not them or us, spoke of it outside the building's walls. Concealed in the center of the city in a plain, tan-brick building that could have been the dentist's or the tax attorney's office, the club was exclusive in the way that too much money made things. We couldn't have joined—not that we wanted to, we often said. Even if *our* fathers had handed us riches from their fathers and their grandfathers before them, made off of the lives and deaths of black and brown bodies, none of us would want to be complicit in such terrible opulence; we only swept up the place.

We took the jobs. Of course we took the jobs. We were citizens with citizens' needs: food and housing and medical care. Our children wanted and we desired they be allowed their want, that they sometimes have it satisfied. We didn't ask for much, much less than the members themselves, only that we might afford to be human, and in this way, the pay, cash in hand, was hard to beat.

Once a month, the members gathered in the night, wearing elaborate half-face masks in the likenesses of pigs and dogs and cats that hid their eyes but left their mouths free. While we poured tart cherry mead, fetched fresh cloth napkins, procured new spoons for ones that had fallen, we observed them: a walrus tipping back raw oysters; a big-eyed cow knifing marmalade onto toast; a peacock shimmering in a gold dress, sloshing pink champagne onto the floor. We cleaned it up. We swept crumbs from the linen. We cleared plates between courses and some of us might have drawn our fingers through ribbons of decorative sauce or nudged unbitten nibbles into the palms of our hands. If we caught one another doing so, we pretended that we hadn't. At every dinner, our faces were bare; the members wanted to know us, though they pretended we had no power. We didn't know that we did. They conversed around us as if speaking through air, and we came to know most intimately what they thought about the world. One night, over fugu ceviche, a jackal said: The Revolution was never about freedom. We just wanted more kings.

They were the kings, so they laughed.

The Supper Club specialized in exotic meats—the dining table raised on a platform, the eating itself the art. The members devoured main courses of stuffed gator over dirty rice, emu in raspberry sauce, anaconda slivered into hearty stew, and slabs of roasted lion they joked came direct from Pride Rock. They declared ortolan passé, though once we witnessed the tiny bodies disappear beneath the further shroud of napkins, and through their wet smacking, heard the crunch of delicate skulls. They were jeweled animals eating lesser animals, and to each other, with our eyes, we communicated our disgust. We did not prepare the food or choose it. Of course, we served them; we did only our jobs. We fed our children and kept the roofs above their heads. We watched the members gorge themselves in January, February, March and April and May. We collected our unmarked envelopes as they licked extravagant gravy from their fingers.

In November, the members cried, Next month must be the rarest! Bigger, better! We deserve! Their mouths always watering for the next meal before they'd finished the last. A panda draped her arm across the gilded chair of a buffalo, her husband, and said, For Christmas let's have something truly special. Maybe the last of something, and us the only ones to taste.

On the night of the last supper, while we set the table with crystal stemware and festooned mistletoe above the archways, we heard the sleepy cries from the kitchen, the shh-shhshing of the chefs. We heard the lullabies, ones that had been sung to us and that we now sang, the melodies cleaving down to our bones. We were angry! Of course we were. We didn't want this. We didn't condone it—but what could we do? We brought the dishes to the table to gasps of nearly erotic anticipation and stepped back and dropped our eyes. If we didn't look, we could still pretend. Their silverware filled the room with music.

My God, we heard a canary say quietly to a sheep, her hands at her mouth. We knew, if they could, they'd eat Him, too.

And afterward, once the floors were clean, the table stripped, the dishes washed and the cutlery polished, once it seemed that the club had never been, we stood in line for our money. As a bonus, a nod to the year of our dedicated service, each of us was given a white bag as we left by the back door. Merry Christmas, the chefs said. Bon appétit. We took the bags; we tucked them under our coats. None of us spoke. What could we say? In the parking lot, stepping into our used cars, avoiding each other's eyes, we shrugged. We excused ourselves. Anyway, we might have thought, haven't we always eaten the young?

# An Almanac of Bones

Kit showed me the Polaroids on the bus after school. They were taken in the woods behind her grandfather's farm—tree roots thick as branches disappearing into black dirt, everything dappled in moss; pine needles on the ground; the kind of evening light hobbyists thrilled to paint. The skull was half-buried in leaves and a Kit-sized shadow crossed into the edges of the frame. In another photo, she'd uncovered it, and her hand rested on its top. In the pictures, her nails were tangerine, the now-chipped polish glossy and intact. The bus bumped along, knocking us gently together.

Across the aisle, two eighth graders were kissing, slouched down so the bus driver couldn't see. The boy's hands were out of sight, most likely on the small of her back, tracing the pinkish skin underneath her shirt. I imagined thought bubbles above their heads. His read: *I am so cool* and hers:

*I hope this looks cool.* I watched them like I wasn't watching them, like Kit pretended not to watch them, and counted to twenty-seven before they took a break.

"Sylvie, what kind of animal is this?" Kit asked when they were through, as if she were only waiting for me to speak.

I examined the skull. There was no lower jaw and half of the right eye socket was missing. The teeth were impressively jagged, some broken, and the head torpedo-shaped. This always delighted me, how extraordinary things could look outside their flesh—it could have been a Martian or a baby raptor head. I told Kit I needed more data.

"Come back to my house," I said, and at my stop we both got off.

It was a dry autumn day, the sky high and clear. The path to my house was a long dirt trail surrounded by a field of grass and what passed for hills in Florida. Sometimes I rolled down those hills with my arms stiff at my sides, as if I were an unstoppable wheel going bigger places than here.

We went inside and left our backpacks in the foyer, stretched our shoulders and shrugged the school day off—the algebra question we got wrong in front of everyone, the pizza sauce we dripped on our white shirts, the way the boys were kissing all our classmates, but not us. My grandmother waited in the kitchen.

"Sylvie," she called, and Kit and I went in and sat at the island where she fed us tuna sandwiches and tall glasses of Florida-style SunnyD. I loved that about my grandmother, that she was never thrown. I brought home a friend and she didn't bat an eye, made an extra sandwich as if she were planning to anyway. That's how I imagined she got me—that my mother dropped me off and my grandmother just shrugged and raised me as if, all along, she had wanted a second child.

My grandmother was still beautiful, even with what she called her marionette lines and the permanent crinkles at the corners of her eyes. She said gratitude kept her young. She wasn't particularly tall, but the way she carried herself, you'd think she was at least ten feet. No one could look down on my grandmother. She had warm hands, a thoughtful face, and long silver hair she wore in a braid down her back. I hoped I would be like that someday: my hair over my shoulder, posture immaculate, fixing sandwiches in my own home in a man's Hawaiian shirt.

"Are you joining us for the moon festival?" she asked Kit.

Kit blushed and ducked her head. "My mom won't let me."

"That's too bad," my grandmother said, and turned to the sink to put away dishes she'd already washed. "What about you, Sylvie? Up for it tonight?"

It was a school night, but of course I was. I'd never been a good sleeper, and my grandmother knew this. *Everything is as it is,* she was always saying, which I took to mean I could go to bed when I was tired.

"Duh," I said, my mouth full. I scarfed the rest of my sandwich and drained my glass so we could figure out what Kit's animal was.

"Your mother called," my grandmother said as I picked the last crumbs from my plate with the tip of a spit-slick finger. "She's temping at the hospital while she's in town. She might come by."

"Mmm," I said, and then to Kit, "Come on." She thanked my grandmother for the food and we thundered up the hardwood stairs to my room. It was exactly how I'd left it that morning: bed unmade, my dirty socks hanging from the hamper, the window wide open, letting in sun and air. I hit play on my Sony Boombox, and TLC's "Unpretty" bumped from the speakers, a song that, lately, I kept on repeat.

"What are the festivals like? Is your mother really a gypsy?" Kit asked rapid-fire, flouncing down on my bed. I turned my back to her and squashed my clothes into the hamper, straightened the books on my desk, as if I cared about such things.

Kit told me that this word—*gypsy*—was something she'd overheard her parents say. Apparently, they discussed my situation often while she eavesdropped from her room. Her parents had a Christmas-card family: Mom, Dad, Kit and her little brother. All of them well-groomed, smiling practiced white grins they tacked up on their walls for visitors to see. Kit's mom sold Mary Kay at parties to other moms wearing identical cable-knit sweaters and the latest yoga pants, and she served store-bought guacamole in authentic Native American pottery she ordered online. Every time I saw her, she smiled at me with all her teeth, and the silver fillings in her back molars winked. When I heard "gypsy," I pictured someone beautiful and dark and charming, but the way Kit repeated the word made it clearly a slur. Like whatever her parents meant when they said it, was lesser than them. She said "festival" that same way.

"What does your mother say about the festivals?" I asked Kit, flexing my nails into my palm.

Kit laughed, and propped back on my bed. "She doesn't like them. Every time I come over here, she asks if your grandmother walks around naked."

I felt my anger prickle in my fingertips, jab underneath my ribs. How could anyone judge my grandmother, let alone Kit's mother? I wanted to stare down her mother's generic face and tell her yes, we walked around naked. And we dipped ourselves in blood. I wanted to tell Kit exactly what I thought about her mother, but she was nearly the only girl in school who didn't think I was weird, who had interest in the games I liked to play. I pretended not to be offended by her questions, as if the implications of either topic were lost on me.

"They're magic," I said about the festivals. "You're missing out."

I said nothing about my mother, whom I called Helen to her face. I didn't talk about her with anyone. She was mine to talk about, or not, and I was the only one allowed to think badly of her.

She'd left me, two years old with my newly constructed sentences, *Bye-bye Mommy!*, to travel the world. I only saw her when she drifted home—when she was tired or missing something—on a schedule regulated by a system only she could understand; that she made out in a bird's flight south or a certain turn of tide. A Helen's Almanac for when to appear in her daughter's life. She liked to tell me about all that she'd done. She had cleaned yachts for a living, chased boys across continents, cut paths on Antigua's smoking mountains with a silver blade. Once she swam with baby humpback whales. She told me of a time she walked barefoot up Mount Sinai to the burning bush, fresh blisters on her toes, and bowed down to it on the summit. She told all her friends she'd heard the voice of God. *Do you know what He said?* she'd ask them, eyes shining, and everyone always asked, *What?* leaning in, greedy for secrets. *Nothing*, she'd say. Sometimes the voice of God was silence.

I told myself I didn't begrudge my mother these experiences; how could I? We barely knew each other, if at all.

Kit and I turned toward my neatly labeled shelves. I was interested in discarded things—dead scalp flakes, toenail rinds, animal remains. I pressed cast-off flower petals onto yellowed sheet music. Rolled snake skins into opaque scrolls and corked them inside specimen bottles. In this realm, I was the expert, and Kit deferred to me. With the photos on the floor at the center of the room, we went through all my bones: wolf, cougar, goat, and sheep. There were chipmunks and rabbits, a viper and a blue jay. A tortoise. We arranged their heads around Kit's pictures like totems, as if maybe their spirits were hanging out somewhere near my room—though I'd had most shipped from faraway places off the internet—and could be summoned to help us solve this mystery. They watched us arranging the sum of their parts, eternal grins indecipherable. There was something dark in their look, something true. We gathered my entire supply, tossing down femurs, scapulae, one rodent clavicle, and yellowed vertebrae like strange doorknobs. We beat upon the skulls with the ribs from a porcupine, popping our skinny hips to the graveyard music. I combed Kit's hair with a bear's phalanges; she placed a crown of thoracic spikes on mine.

After a while, we got tired of searching and thought: *maybe fox*. It didn't matter if we were right. Sometimes, it wasn't about naming the bones we found; we rejoiced in the questions as much as the answers. It was enough, for us, to hold them against our skin, run their particular shapes across our mouths and taste that something remained—a sweet flavor, dust-dry.

We left the bones where they lay and called numbers on my yellow daisy phone. My grandmother had a second line installed so the internet wouldn't tie up her main. When she wasn't using it, it was mine; when she was, a horrible robotic blatting and thick static filled the receiver—the sounds of connection.

We called for the time, though we had nowhere to be. We phoned a free dating service that allowed us to skip through chatrooms by pressing pound or star and pretended to be girls older than we were. We laughed when men told us what they would do to us—spastic, ugly giggles that made our stomachs ache. They would treat us like princesses; they would kiss our feet; they would slather us in honey and lick the cracks of our succulent asses. We never said what we would do.

But Kit and I figured we should be prepared, so we practiced giving hickeys on our own arms, then receiving hickeys from each other. Kit left controlled blooms beneath my collarbone, but I sucked her left shoulder splotchy red. I imagined Kit as the dark-skinned boy who wore tucked-in shirts and smiled kindly at me at school, and we practiced kissing on the lips. I was an eighth-grade girl on a school bus, basking in shy admiration.

"I've got to go," Kit said around five, and waved good-bye. Her sweater covered up our practice work. My grandmother's voice drifted up the stairs, offering Kit a ride home, but she said, "No, thank you." She'd walk. Exhausted from our searching, our pretending, from all our nervous laughing, I lay down on my bed and watched the sky in its singular mass of blue.

I thought about the last time I had seen my mother, when she showed up last year in a gauzy black dress and burgundy leather boots, as if for a concert instead of a daughter's eleventh birthday. I was surprised to see her. Usually she appeared a couple of weeks before or after a birthday, never quite getting the timing right. The year before that, I hadn't seen her at all.

At the front door, she'd held up a small box wrapped in gold paper.

"Earrings," she'd told me, rattling the present before placing it in my palm. "A girl should have some jewelry." Helen wore none.

She grabbed a bottle of red wine from my grandmother's cabinet and brought it to my room with a glass already full, wedging herself onto my bed that used to be hers. I sat with her and we faced each other, our knees pulled up. She told me about how she and her high school friends used to spray-paint their bodies bronze and pose as statues at the park, copying famous figures, unmoving for hours while one of them shook a ball cap at whomever happened by. She said on weekends they used to rake it in, but paid most of their earnings to a kid they knew with a fake ID who'd buy them packs of light beer and cigarettes. The emptier the bottle got, the further into the past she went.

"Do you have a boyfriend?"

"I'm eleven, Helen," I'd said.

She told me about when she was eleven. How she'd ride her bicycle to her boyfriend's house, who was eleven too, and give him head in his backyard, knees scraping against the hand-poured slab of his basketball court, bone on concrete—the tender patches of ashy skin those encounters left. She said his come tasted like nothing. "Not like later," she'd said, touching the soft hairs at the nape of her neck. She wasn't looking at me; she didn't seem to be looking at anything. She was somewhere inside herself. "Later, everything tastes like something."

My grandmother appeared in the doorway. "Cake's ready," she said to me, but she was looking at my mother. "Why don't you go on downstairs and get the stuff for frosting? I'll be down in a minute and we'll ice it once it cools."

"Yes ma'am," I said, realizing she'd overheard some of our conversation and didn't want it to continue. I didn't mind leaving; I thought I already knew how sex worked, anyway. I had seen the glossy torn-out pages other girls brought in from their mothers' *Cosmos*, had watched a boy at school stick his hand up the leg of a classmate's rolled-up gym shorts. Nothing was said to the boy, but she was written up for dress code. I didn't need Helen to tell me.

I pretended to leave, but lurked just outside the doorway, holding my breath, eager to see how Helen handled reprimand. Instead I saw my grandmother finger-comb my mother's hair. Watched her wrap her arms around her, and Helen snuggle in. In the kitchen, while I slammed down bowls and dye and piping bags, I wondered why she'd even bothered to have me. I estimated the number of boyfriends she might have had over the years, the many children she had swallowed as seeds. How painless. I wished I'd been eaten, too.

Later that day, when some of my grandmother's friends were visiting, my mother sat in the tree swing facing the field—all that land, the gentle green slopes—swaying softly, her wine glass refilled. The women looked on from the porch, and one friend said to the other, "That girl," and rolled her eyes. She said it low so my grandmother wouldn't hear, but I heard, and thought, *If she's still a girl, when can any of us be women?*

I pictured my mother as a child, dressed in frills and lace, a red bow in her hair bigger than her head. She had a sticky, lollipop mouth instead of a wine bottle and glass and, sitting in that same swing, she pumped her legs, taking herself higher and higher, so high that her nose grazed the green of the tree, and the leaves all fell around her, turning red, turning brown, leaving the shriveled skeletons of their former selves underneath her feet. She was laughing, unaware she was about to swing into the sky, about to be lost, a pinprick among clouds. She didn't call my name. She didn't say words at all. There was only her in her dress and her smile, swinging into blue, then pink-orange, then gray-purple into black.

My grandmother's face hung above me, radiant and calm; I must have fallen asleep. She brushed a hand across the trail of self-inflicted love marks on my arms. "Are you ready?" she asked, and then helped me dress—I chose a skirt of such pale pink it was almost white, my grandmother a gown of teal chiffon. Then, wreathed in flowers, crowns of lavender and orange carnations like puffs of colored dust, we stepped into the yard.

The field had been transformed in the time I slept. My grandmother and her friends had set up a tent underneath which tables were laid with wine and bread and fruit, slices of yellow pear and nectarines, black grapes large as pinballs, hunks of soft cheese staged attractively atop banana leaves. Lanterns and paper streamers hung from the porch and every branch, and a bonfire crackled. The field was bathed in all manner of light—soft light, twinkling light, roaring red light. Someone played the ukulele, someone else a tambourine.

There were women everywhere—my grandmother's friends and strangers from the next town over, some from even farther than that. There were women who taught children, women who filed papers, women who cleaned toilets.

Businesswomen, pleasure women, women who'd married, and those that never did. Women in flowers, in grass skirts, in braids, in beads, women in only their skins. Old women, new women, tall women. Women hugging and singing and running and praying, women drinking in the night.

A forest of women undulating under a full harvest moon.

My grandmother left my side to dance, and I walked the grass among them. During these festivals, she didn't hold my hand. It was up to me to navigate my own way, and I took this as a sign of trust. I could handle myself; I would be okay. I thought about Kit and her mother inserted into the scene, their bloodless faces, how small and lost they would be.

I wandered toward a group telling stories by the fire, sitting cross-legged on the ground. They beckoned me to join them and spoke about their ghosts—a sister slain, a son dead in the womb. A grandmother who'd never made it over to this country, and all that remained of her was a pair of kidskin gloves. "It's rarely cold enough," the granddaughter said, "for me to wear them." The woman next to her reached over and squeezed her hand; she'd painted gold circles in a line across her cheeks. I couldn't guess her age, but she was older, darker-skinned, more beautiful than me. She said that she was fortunate, she hadn't lost a loved one, not yet. She told us you could be a ghost in your own life, and sometimes that was worse. I sat among them, enraptured by their stories, realizing for the first time that every one of us was a link stretching back, mother to daughter to mother, in an unbroken chain from the center of time, connected by milk and blood. Suddenly it felt urgent, that empty space between my grandmother and me.

"Tell your story," the women encouraged each other. I closed my eyes and tried to picture mine, not my past, but something like a future. I was underground, beyond rock and root, stones like bones drawing me deeper, still deeper, until I was in the yellow molten center of the planet. I passed through it, hair and muscle and everything else I thought I was sloughing off until I saw the true shape of myself without my skin. I was a glorious creature, spare and glowing.

Then, piercing through that vision I heard the sound of my own voice. "Sylvia," it said, and I realized it wasn't me. I opened my eyes and saw Helen standing in front of me, appearing as if from the smoke. She wore green scrubs and a fatigue-darkened grin. "I found you," she said. She shifted her purse to the crook of her arm and held out her hand. I said nothing. I was always there, right where she'd left me.

I stood up from the circle and put my hand in hers. "I'm hungry," she said, and led me toward the house, leaving the sound of women behind us—crying happy, laughing sad. The sounds of connection.

At the front door, I stopped her. My grandmother used to tell me that full moons brought out impish creatures, magical beasts that traveled only by its light. I glared at Helen. All that time she'd been away. Her hunger. I wanted to be sure. "Are you a vampire?" I asked. I wouldn't be the one to invite danger in. My mother shuffled through her bag and very seriously showed me her reflection in a heart-shaped compact.

"Not yet," she said.

I swung the door wide, letting it hit the wall, and stomped upstairs to sit on the edge of my bed, swinging my legs, waiting for her, because even though she wasn't necessarily here for me, I knew she'd come.

She brought the rest of the tuna salad, eating it straight from the Tupperware, and a glass of milk. "Drink this," she said, and handed the glass to me.

"Why?"

"Isn't that what mothers do? Bring milk to their unsleeping children?"

I said nothing. The milk glowed blue-white in the glass.

"It's good for the bones," she tried.

"Actually, that's not true," I told her, glad to disagree.

"It was true when I was your age." She didn't speak again until I'd grudgingly taken a sip. She pointed with her fork to the bones on the floor. "What's that?"

"Coyote femur," I said. My grandmother had brought it back from a trip to Arizona.

Helen laughed. "Good lord, you're just like me."

I bristled at that, baby hair on my arms standing on end—how would she know what I was like? I thought of Kit's ready-made mom, and looked at Helen the way she would: gypsy, lesser than.

"My friend's mom would never let her come to the moon festivals."

She looked at me, and the center of her eyes were black as grapes. "What does your friend's mother do?" she asked, like she already knew the answer and it was laughable.

"Stays," I said. Maybe I imagined it, but I thought I heard her inhale, a small sound, like a flinch. She asked, "Is that what makes a good mother?"

She was the one with all the answers, woman of the world. I clutched the glass tight in my hands, bracing myself. "How would I know anything about mothers?"

A beat, and then Helen laughed—raspy, sad—and speared an onion, crunched it hard between her teeth. "Domesticity is for animals," she said. "And really, not even them." I pictured Kit's family as a skulk of foxes, their skulls all lined up and proper on someone's fireplace mantle—daddy, momma, and two babies—unfamiliar to one another without their silky pelts.

"Everything is as it is," my mother said. She smiled at me and it reached her eyes too. There was something dark there, something true. "You learn to be who you are, or you die as someone else. It's simple."

It didn't seem simple, certainly not then, sitting in silence while my resentment swelled between us. Years later, I would come to see those offerings—the earrings, the milk, her honesty—as her way of asking for my acceptance. She couldn't ask me for forgiveness. She was too herself to apologize for her nature.

"Finish that," she said, tapping my glass, and of course I did. We were tree and fruit. No matter how long she was gone, my body always knew.

She took the empties—the bowl, the glass—and disappeared down the stairs. I listened to her footfalls until they grew soft, until they faded entirely and I knew she had gone to the spare room to sleep before she left for wherever it was her almanac told her to go next.

Left alone with the animal remains still scattered on the rug and my belly full of milk, I sent myself to sleep. Told my own bedtime stories. I pictured women dancing, women spinning. Helen flying into black.

I felt my bones fashioning themselves into something like her: sturdy, sharp, and too exquisite to be human. In a hundred years, archaeologists or curious children would dig me up, brushing earth from my splintered femurs, studying my humerus for a hint at the joke. They would never quite get it because they couldn't see the whole: my fierce weirdness or the restless current that circled my spine. They would wonder what kind of animal I'd been as they photographed my partial skeleton and counted my grinning teeth. They would gild my bones in bronze and hang them on walls behind glass, and men would pay money to see.

# Acknowledgments
## A.K.A
## Love Notes

Writing is a solitary practice—until it's absolutely not. Without the encouragement, guidance, and energy of so many magnificent humans, this book simply wouldn't be. I won't be perfect here; I know there are names I might miss. But if, during the writing of this book, you have ever read for me, written for me, fed me, held space for me, laughed or cried with me, know that you have my thanks, and that for me, gratitude is a special kind of love.

So much love to Meredith Kaffel Simonoff, my "here for any and all" super-agent, who took me on at the beginning when she definitely didn't have to—for all of her support, intellect, and insight. For her heart. You are above and beyond anything I could have ever hoped for. Love to my Grove editor, Katie Raissian: same-spirited, big-laughing, art-as-life *genius*, who saw this book and understood it at its core, and who most importantly saw me, and fought so hard for us both. Big thanks to my Atlantic editor, James Roxburgh, who could make a bestselling book out of his emails, who talked to me straight and treated these stories with attention that was at once tender and serious. The four of us make the dreamiest team.

Thank you to everyone who ushered this book from computer pages to physical object in the world: the entire team at Grove Atlantic and Atlantic Books, especially Deb Seager, Judy Hottensen, Kait Astrella, and Poppy Mostyn-Owen; thank you to Gretchen Mergenthaler, and to Kelly Winton and Helen Crawford-White for designing such delicious covers; many thanks to the production team, the copyeditors, and the proofreaders: Julia Berner-Tobin, Sal Destro, Cassie McSorley, Brenna McDuffie, and Kirsten Giebutowski—y'all are rockstars; and thank you to Jacey Mitziga and Hanna Kenne for keeping things running smoothly.

Thank you to the program of Creative Writing at the University of Wisconsin-Madison where most of these stories were first written, with special thanks to Jesse Lee Kercheval, Sean Bishop, Amaud Jamaul Johnson, and Amy Quan Barry. To Judith Claire Mitchell, thank you for being the first champion of my work, for telling me when it wasn't working, but especially for telling me when it was (#vivalajudy!); love and thanks to my fiction cohort, who saw these stories in their rawest form and spent time with me, talking through the work: Maddy Court, Jack Ortiz, Rodrigo Restrepo (thank you for everything), Carrie Schuettpelz, Jennie Seidewand (additionally, thank you for all the late-night Netflix-binge hangs), and Emily Shetler. I am so grateful to many institutions for the gift of time, space, and financial support: much gratitude to Hedgebrook, the Key West Literary Seminars, Jack Jones Literary Arts, Tin House (special mentions to Lance Cleland, karaoke legend), and the Elizabeth George Foundation. And thank you to the editors of the magazines listed at the front of this book for your gracious attention, and for publishing these stories.

Thanks to these writers I admire greatly for their talent and generosity, and for the early reads, mentorship, and support: Nana Kwame Adjei-Brenyah, Jamel Brinkley, Danielle Evans (with extra thanks for your brilliance at UW), Lauren Groff (thank you for Tin House and beyond), T Kira Madden, and Nafissa Thompson-Spires. This meant everything to me.

To the homies, I would not have wanted to walk this path without you: big love to Michael Lee (we're eating frand!), María Alvarez, Shelley Senai; thank you to TSWT for the early support; Chet'la Sebree, you are a balm in my life—thank you for continually getting me all the way together; and to Sarah Fuchs—these stories have benefited greatly from your sharp eye, your insistence that I could do better. Thank you for everything.

Biggest thanks to my family for their belief in me, and nothing but love, gratitude, and respect to my mom and dad for teaching me as best they could how to live a life.

Finally, thank you to Jason Moniz, who has provided me with unflagging support for the last decade, who has grown up and failed and flown with me; who with just a look, knows exactly what I mean. Thank you for seeing the goodness in me when I couldn't see it in myself.

GROVE PRESS

Reading Group Guide

by Taylor Victoria Michael

# Milk Blood Heat

Dantiel W. Moniz

## ABOUT THIS GUIDE

We hope that these discussion questions will enhance your reading group's exploration of Dantiel W. Moniz's *Milk Blood Heat*. They are meant to stimulate discussion, offer new viewpoints, and enrich your enjoyment of the book.

More reading group guides and additional information, including summaries, author tours, and author sites for other fine Grove Atlantic titles may be found on our website, groveatlantic.com.

**QUESTIONS FOR DISCUSSION**

In these stories, Moniz explores many forms of kinship, someone a character may feel beholden to or connected through, "something beneath the skin" (2), or "by milk and blood" (195). Discuss these bonds and how characters navigate a duty to the self, versus a duty to someone else.

---

In "Milk Blood Heat," Kiera and Ava play a morbid game of questions in which they imagine their deaths. " 'How would it be to drown in a pool?' 'How would it be for a man to slice you up and hide you under his mattress?' " (7). Why do you think these prepubescent girls fixate on death just as their lives and bodies are starting to change?

---

Moonlight appears as a recurring image in the book. Discuss the ways moonlight illuminates what some characters hide in daylight.

---

In "Feast," Rayna struggles to heal from a miscarriage. Discuss the ways in which Rayna negotiates or processes her "common pain" (28). How does she come to understand the cycle of loss and rebirth?

---

Think about the word *luciferous*. Zey comes back to this word many times in "Tongues." How do light and darkness, goodness and evil, interact in this story?

---

Guilt is a theme that connects many of the stories. Characters are made to feel or not feel guilty for a host of reasons and circumstances. Talk about the place of guilt and gender in some of the conflicts explored.

---

Fred, one of few male protagonists in the collection, doesn't see Gloria clearly in "The Loss of Heaven." And Gloria, who struggles most in the story, at times fades into the background. Discuss Fred as a main character, and how he relates to his wife as she deals with her diagnosis.

---

Discuss the role of food and cooking in "The Hearts of Our Enemies."

---

In "Outside the Raft," the adults around Shayla and Tweet have opinions about who of the two cousins is touched with darkness. Discuss how the adult's opinions of the girls influence their actions. What does Shayla learn about darkness? What does Tweet learn about light?

---

In "Snow," discuss Trinity's yearning for touch and how it becomes both the source of and also salvation from some of her doubts.

---

In "Necessary Bodies," we see Billie navigate pressure from her mother to have children. Discuss Billie's reservations about having a child and how both her environment and her own inclinations influence her decisions.

---

Cecilia wonders "what it's like to be so comfortable in your own body, you don't try to mask the scents of its functioning but instead make a profit off them" (168). Discuss how Cecilia navigates her relationship to her body in "Thicker Than Water," particularly in light of her familial history and relationships with her father, brother, and mother. How is memory played out in this story? What impact does memory have on each of the characters?

---

"Exotics" is the only story told from a first-person plural perspective. How does the "we" add to this collection? Who is a part of the "we"? Who might be excluded?

---

In the final story, "An Almanac of Bones," Sylvia witnesses "A forest of women undulating under a full harvest moon" (194) and finds solace, strength, and stories among these women. Discuss the ways this multitudinousness of womanhood gives Sylvia a perspective on motherhood that her friend might not have. How does Sylvia's own mother impact these perspectives?

---

## SUGGESTIONS FOR FURTHER READING

*Secret Life of Church Ladies* by Deesha Philyaw

*Crooked Hallelujah* by Kelli Jo Ford

*Libertie* by Kaitlyn Greenidge

*Caul Baby* by Morgan Jerkins

*Of Women and Salt* by Gabriela Garcia

*This Close to Okay* by Leesa Cross-Smith

*The Removed* by Brandon Hobson

*Love Is an Ex-Country* by Randa Jarrar

*Milk Fed* by Melissa Broder

*The Kindest Lie* by Nancy Johnson